STEALING FOREVER

A.R. ROSE

Edited By: Virginia Tesi Carey

Proofread by: The Cauldron Author Services & Ellyn L.

Cover background and character art by: @krizhanskaya

Paperback ISBN: 978-1-968791-00-1

OTHER TITLES BY A.R. ROSE

Ridgewood Series
*Between the Flames**
*Wicked Games We Play**
Marked By Cain

Standalones
Wreck Me
Only One Night
I Really Can't Stay

Twisted Heroes
Siren
A Captain So Callous and Cruel

With a Kiss
Sins of Sorrow
The Sinners
Sins of Bliss

**eBooks and paperbacks unpublished for rewrites. Original story available in audiobook.*

AUTHORS NOTE

Stealing Forever is the first book in a series of interconnected standalones that is intended for an adult audience. Reader discretion is advised. Stealing Forever contains content that may be triggering for some, as well as sexually explicit content.

Your mental health matters. For a full list of content warnings, please visit www.authorarrose.com/content-warnings.

To the readers who'd like to catch themselves a coach, this one's for you. We're all Coach Declan's good girls.

PROLOGUE

Declan

Three months ago

"I quit, Mr. Lane. I'm sorry."

"I—?" My nanny is quitting? I haven't even been home for thirty seconds. Hell, I'm not even one step inside of the front door, my heavy backpack's still slung over my shoulder and there's mud caked on the bottom of my slides that I haven't had a chance to kick off yet. "What?"

My bag hits the floor with a heavy thud, and I scrub my hands down my face in frustration, or maybe it's exhaustion. Probably both, it's been a damn day.

She pushes off the couch to her feet and folds the blanket she'd been sitting under. "I'm sorry. I know this is abrupt, but I didn't want to lose the courage. I just can't do these late nights, and I know the season is starting soon, so you'll be traveling. I'm just realizing this isn't the gig for me."

Fuck. It took me weeks to find Liza—now I'll have to start all over again.

Swallowing the lump in my throat, I nod curtly. "Understood. Any chance you have a referral for a replacement?"

A friend? A family member? *Fucking anyone?*

"I'll put some feelers out. I'm *really* sorry, Mr. Lane."

"It's fine," I grumble. It's not fine, but what else am I supposed to say?

She bends over in front of me to pick up her purse by the door, and I avert my eyes, glancing around my living room instead.

"What time did she go to sleep?" A glance at my watch tells me it's nearing eleven. No wonder Liza is quitting—I told her I'd be home by nine. She isn't a live-in nanny, and I'm sure my constant tardiness drives her crazy. In my defense, I warned her prior to her taking the job.

She smiles, shifting her hand to curl around the strap of her bag as she readies herself to leave. "Seven-thirty sharp. I did a load of her laundry earlier, but didn't wash her stuffed animals since she wanted to sleep with Snug-Bug. I also bought new berries at the market today, and they're washed and ready in the fridge. Your credit card is on the counter."

"Thank you, Liza."

"No problem. Sorry things didn't work out on my end."

"I understand." Do I, though? She's only been with us for two months. Sure, my time management sucks, but when she interviewed to nanny for a single dad she should have known. Unfortunately, things have been a lot busier than I anticipated they'd be when I hired her, but I'm gearing up for my first year as *head coach*.

And although I'm no spring chicken at thirty-six years old, I'm the youngest the Bridge Point Bears have ever had. Which is why I've been pulling such long hours to prove myself, not only to the managerial staff, but to my team.

Because goddamn, do I have my work cut out for me with these guys.

Opening the front door, I hold it for her. "Thanks for everything."

"Please tell Sailor I said bye." She gives me a small wave, then walks out the front door, never once looking back.

I watch and make sure she makes it safely into her car parked on the street, then shut the door. Slumping against it, I mutter a curse.

Finding a nanny to work for a single dad is hard enough—I know what it's like for women these days, and I don't fault them for being leery of men.

Hell, if I were female, I'd be cautious, too. So the second they learn there is no missus, half of the candidates lose interest in scheduling an interview to meet me and my three-year-old daughter.

Then, it's a game of Goldilocks to find the right fit for us.

I *really* don't want to go through this again, but I have no other choice.

Sailor deserves far more than a revolving door of babysitters, she deserves someone who loves her and will give her the best care, day in and day out, when that person can't be me.

And I'm determined to find the perfect woman for the job, no matter what.

"C'mon, Sailor, Daddy's going to be late!" The clock on the wall taunts me, reminding me we should have left ten minutes ago. My meeting with the Bears' execs is in less than thirty minutes, and I need to make it across Bridge Point in the next twenty.

"But I want Snug-Bug!" Sailor stomps her little foot on the ground, her arms crossed with a sour look on her face.

"Snug-Bug *just* went into the dryer, Sail. He'll be nice and clean by the time we get home."

Her eyes fill with tears, and she gives me the goddamn

pouty lip that makes my heart tear to shreds every single time.

"How about a cookie?" I scoop her up, succumbing to bribery. With Sailor on my hip, I open the pantry and use one hand to pop the lid on the plastic container full of Oreos. Her little grabby hands swipe it from me, so I grab another, sticking it between my teeth, then shift one to the hand I'm holding her with.

With Sailor distracted, I bolt to the front door, stopping only to pick up my backpack and lock the house up. When I've finally wrangled my daughter into her car seat, I haul ass through town—safely of course, but as fast as I can.

She isn't *supposed* to come with me, but since my nanny quit last night, my only option is to bring her.

The sound of *Ms. Rachel* floats through the car from her tablet, and I hope to God the device keeps her busy during this meeting.

Today is not a day for no screen time.

Traffic is light, thankfully, and I pull into a parking spot adjacent to the stadium and hang my parking permit with minutes to spare. It leaves me enough time to get us into the conference room that overlooks the ballpark.

Depositing her into a leather office chair that engulfs her tiny frame, I prop her tablet in her lap, lay her favorite blanket next to her, and hand her the last Oreo. She doesn't even look up at me by the time I've frantically situated her, but I can't say the same for the audience I now have.

When I take my seat, all eyes are on me.

Considering this is only my second meeting with the executives, my heart is hammering. Hopefully, I'm not canned for bringing my kid.

"You brought your kid?" Blake Bradley, the team's owner, scoffs, ironically echoing my thoughts. His eyes scrutinize me, but I hold my head high. He's not much older than I am, but he's the one looking out of place, wearing a three-piece suit at a ballpark. Fuckin' billionaires.

"My nanny quit on me last night." I lean back, draping my arm over the armrests of mine and Sailor's chairs.

"Oof. That's a toughy." Clive, the team's accountant, taps his pen against the lined-yellow notepad in front of him.

"I'll find another." *Eventually.* I'm not holding out hope that this will be a speedy process.

The conversation gets cut short when Blake begins speaking about the upcoming season, potential trades, and finances.

Around the oblong conference table sit the most important men behind the scenes for the Bridge Point Bears: the owner, the in-house lawyers, our accountant, and, of course, the coaches, myself as the head coach *and* manager, and my four assistant coaches.

Our team is the strongest we've ever been *behind-the-*

scenes, and if we secure the trades Blake's hoping we do, we'll be a force on the field as well.

For years, the Bears have been the underdogs in the majors, but since Blake Bradley bought the team two years ago, things have been looking up significantly. With loads of cash at his disposal, he's dumped it into higher salaries, better trade offers, and incredible upgrades to an already brand new stadium.

My promotion came at the perfect time, and I'm grateful for the previous coach's glowing recommendation prior to retirement. I was a shoo-in, having worked for the Bears since I was eighteen. Baseball's been my life since I was four and started Little League. It's in my blood. In my DNA.

I eat, sleep, and *breathe* baseball.

Just being a player for the Bears, or any other team, would've never been enough for me.

I wanted it *all*. I wanted to coach. Be the *head coach*.

And now I am.

An hour and a half, and a pissed off three-year-old later, we're all clearing the room, done for the day.

"Hey, Lane, you got a moment?" Clive pushes his wire-framed glasses further up his nose, stepping around the table closer to me.

"That's not Daddy's name. Daddy's name is Declan." Sailor's nose scrunches, then she looks back down at her tablet, now blaring *Bluey*.

Clive chuckles, shifting his shoulder bag while smiling down at my girl. "Yes, yes, you're right, little one. Sometimes we call your dad by your last name, though." His eyes meet mine. "I might have an answer to your nanny problem."

"Oh?" My backpack hits my shoulders roughly as I toss it on, listening while preparing to leave.

"Why?" Sailor looks up at Clive with confusion. I pick her up and settle her in my arms.

The old man smiles in amusement at Sailor, then shifts his gaze back to me. "I recently rented one of my townhouses to a young woman who's getting her masters through Ridgewood U. Very sweet gal. She mentioned how she wanted to find a job working with kids, since her degrees are in education. She currently works in retail. Anyway, I could contact her to see if she'd babysit for you."

"I really need more of a nanny than a babysitter. You know how grueling the on-season schedule can be."

Clive swishes his hand in my direction as he looks down the curve of his nose to his phone's screen. He roughly taps a few times before bringing it to his ear.

"You're calling her *now*?" I shift Sailor's weight and use my other hand to adjust my backpack.

"No better time than the present—oh! Hi, Hailey. How are you?" He listens intently, nodding as the woman talks.

I know absolutely nothing about this girl. Not her name—although, I guess it's Hailey—her age, or if she even lives in Bridge Point.

"Clive, it's fine. I can just put out an ad," I gruffly whisper, embarrassment flickering through me.

He ignores me. "Glad to hear it. I'm thrilled you're settling in. Hey—question. You'd said you wanted to work with the youngsters. Any interest in being a nanny?"

It feels like time halts while we both wait for her response, although I can't hear their conversation.

A smile breaks out on Clive's face. "That's wonderful! The coach for the Bears is looking for someone to help with his daughter. Hold on, I'll put you on speaker." He jams his finger against the screen, then holds the device flat on his palm. "Hailey, I have Declan here. Let me catch him up to speed."

Because the conversation is so complex?

"Hailey said she loves to work with kids and is interested in talking to you more about watching Sailor."

"Hey, Declan," Hailey's soft and sensual voice flits through the phone. It stirs something inside of me that I immediately ignore.

"Hi, Hailey. I'm so sorry, Clive and I are catching you off guard."

"No worries at all! So you're in the market for a nanny? How old is your daughter?"

"Sailor is three. She goes to preschool a couple days a

week, but my hours with the team are all over the place, and I could use the extra help." I *don't* tell her my last nanny quit on me because she hated my inconsistent schedule. "Clive mentioned you're getting your masters, though, and I, uh—"

On instinct, my fingers sweep through my overgrown hair. Fuck, this suddenly feels incredibly awkward.

Hailey laughs, probably sensing the tension radiating off me through the phone. "My classes are all online, so an unpredictable schedule is not a problem."

"Okay, great. It's probably a good idea for you to come to the house, then we can discuss everything, and you can get a feel for Sailor. See if it's a good fit."

Glancing up, my eyes meet Clive's again. He has a wide smile on his face and nods enthusiastically, giving a thumbs-up.

For some inexplicable reason, my chest tightens when I look back down at the phone, completely unaware that less than ten words would be the start of life as I know it changing forever.

"Sure! I'd love to meet you both. How's tomorrow?"

CHAPTER ONE
Hailey

"No, wait! Don't grab that, it's—"

The bag of flour hits the kitchen floor with a heavy *crash*, going everywhere, and leaving the air clouded in an explosion of hazy white.

"—going to fall." Sighing, I bend over to pick up a now crying Sailor. Her thumb immediately goes into her mouth for comfort as I pat her back. "It's okay, it was an accident."

Flour is *everywhere*—a full Costco-sized ten-pound bag more than half emptied on the tile. Sailor's covered in it, as am I, and I know it's going to be a disaster to clean.

"C'mon, let's get you into the tub." The cookies can wait. So can the mess.

Turning off the oven, the sounds of keys rattling in the lock pull my attention to the front door. *Of course he's home early, the* one *night.*

Seconds later, my boss's face comes into view as he steps into the house. He's wearing his Bears T-shirt and hat, with his overgrown hair peeking past the sides, and a heavy backpack thrown over his shoulder. He takes that thing everywhere.

When Declan Lane sees his daughter and me, his grin slips as his eyes rake over us. "What happened?"

Tossing his keys into a basket, he drops his bag before stalking toward us, hands outstretched when he's a couple steps away. Sailor pulls from me and reaches for her dad, nuzzling in his arms when he takes her. Flour transfers, clinging to his black shirt.

"We had a bit of an accident." Embarrassed, I brush my shirt, trying but failing to make myself more presentable. "We were making cookies and the bag of flour took a tumble..."

"Oh no." Declan's eyes widen at Sailor, a smile pulling at the corners of his mouth. "Is the kitchen a big mess?"

She nods her head yes, still sucking her thumb. Gently, he pulls it from her mouth. We've been working together to try and break her of the habit.

"That's okay." He kisses the side of her head. "Accidents happen. Do you want me to give you a bath, or Ms. Hailey?"

"Ms. Hailey," Sailor tells him, shimmying against his hold. He places her on the floor, and she comes back to me and takes my hand. Pride settles in my chest at the simple gesture that means so much.

Before I started working for the Lane family, I was terrified Declan's daughter would be a nightmare, or wouldn't bond with me. There's a reason why his past nanny quit, right? Although the conversation never came up, I'm not daft enough to think I'm the first nanny he's hired.

"I'll clean up the kitchen when I'm finished," I promise Declan as I lead Sailor through their living room.

His only response is a grunt, but that's nothing new. Declan is a good man and an excellent father from what I've seen, but he's not overly chatty. Typically, by the time he gets home, he looks like he's exhausted.

Once I have Sailor bathed and in her jammies, I settle her on the couch and put a movie on, then ready myself to deal with the mess in the kitchen.

Only, when I step around the counter island, the floor is spotless. In fact, the whole kitchen is completely clean.

A beeping catches me off guard, causing me to jump, slamming my hand against my chest. Turning, I realize Declan put the cookies in the oven.

My heart flips.

Pulling them out, I transfer the delicious treats onto a metal cooling rack before sliding the next batch in.

When I turn around, Declan's leaning against the wall, his arms crossed over his chest, watching me. His hair is a mess from wearing a hat all day, curling around his ears, and he's filthy—his T-shirt and jeans have dirt—and now flour—clinging to them.

Swallowing hard, I avert my gaze and pretend that I'm not insanely interested in him, and turn to clean a non-existent messy spot on the counter.

I shouldn't be this attracted to him. For one, he's eleven years older than me. *And* he's my boss. *And* a single dad. And my *boss*.

"You didn't have to clean up this giant mess." My voice is a lot breathier than it should be as I scrub the already sparkling stove. "I had planned to after Sailor's bath."

"I know, but you've been with her all day. It wasn't a problem."

"You worked all day," I counter. Glancing over my shoulder, I notice he's now leaning against the island, leaning on his forearms. His gaze is dropped to his phone lying on the marble, and whatever he's looking at is making his brows furrow.

Once again, I try not to stare.

I've worked for Declan for almost three months now, and I still haven't built an immunity against his charm. The pathetic thing is, he's not even trying to be charming. He just is.

Even if I was interested in him, which I'm *not*, I'm not his type.

I've seen photos of Sailor's mom. She's stunning.

Petite. Brunette. Tanned skin and chocolate brown eyes. A smile that I just know lights up every room she walks in.

Literally my opposite in every way.

I'm curvy, with flaming red hair, pale skin, and green eyes. I love myself, don't get me wrong, but I know I'm not his cup of tea.

But again, I'm *not* interested in my boss.

"Fucking idiots," Declan mumbles before locking his screen. Pushing it off to the side, he turns his attention my way. "Technically, you're off the clock when I get home, Hailey. The least I can do is help out when I'm here."

"It was a big mess though. So, thank you."

"It was. Pretty sure you two shouldn't be allowed to bake again. If this is what happens when there are cookies, I can't imagine what the kitchen would look like if you girls baked a cake," he teases, and I almost drop the plate in my hand. This is a side to Declan Lane I've never seen before.

Setting the plate in front of him, he grabs a warm chocolate chip cookie, and I shrug. "You won't be saying that after you taste my cookie."

Once the words leave my mouth, I realize I could have chosen better ones. And Declan must realize that, too, because he chokes on said cookie, coughing aggressively.

Heat instantly rises in my skin, embarrassment taking root throughout my entire body.

For several awkward seconds, we simply stare at each other. Then the bastard starts *laughing*.

Kill me. Just kill me now.

Spinning as quickly as possible, I busy myself cleaning up the last part of the kitchen by crumpling the used parchment and throwing it away, then sliding the baking sheet into the drawer under the oven. Declan's hot gaze follows me throughout each movement—I *feel* it, and if I had the ability to melt into a puddle and evaporate, I would. Or I could live out my days as a puddle, too. *Anything* would be better than feeling this heat slither up my neck and onto my face as Declan's hot gaze bores into me. I don't dare turn around and show him how embarrassed I truly am.

I got to get out of here.

"Okay, well, I'll leave you to it!" Springing into action, I toss the towel onto the counter, mentally calculating how quickly I can make it to the front door.

"Hailey, wait." Declan's still laughing, and even though now my back's to him, I scrunch my nose and wave my hand in a weird and hasty departure.

Next to the door, I'm practically falling over as I bounce on one foot, tugging my sneaker onto the other. As I lose balance, my palm slams into the wall.

"Get home safe." Declan's low timbre sneaks up on me from behind, and I suck in a breath. He's so close, I can feel the heat from his body and his breath as it dusts the back of my neck.

For a second, I think he's about to wrap me in his arms, and I forget how to breathe. All I can do is stand still. I squeeze my eyes shut, and wonder if he can hear the gallop of my fight-or-flight heart.

Then, like a movie being unpaused, everything around us snaps back to reality—the blare of the show Sailor's watching, her adorable laugh, the ringing of Declan's phone in the kitchen.

He reaches around me, and twists the doorknob before moving his hand to grip the door, holding it open for me.

Blowing out a shaky breath, I glance up at him from over my shoulder. The look on his face is inexpressive—maybe even a little bored.

My heart sinks.

"Thanks," I mutter, then grab my purse from the bottom shelf of the entryway table and hightail it out the door.

Once I'm in my car, I glance back at the house to make sure Declan is out of view, then slam my head against the headrest. "Stupid, stupid, stupid."

Squeezing my eyes shut for a second, I scoff at myself, shaking my head.

You won't be saying that after you taste my cookie. You utter freaking moron.

Even in the darkness of my car, embarrassment heats my cheeks *again*.

After I've given the engine a few minutes to warm up, I make the drive back to my townhouse, about twenty minutes away.

Bridge Point has bloomed over the last few years, going from a city in need of a serious glow-up to a popular destination, its biggest draw being Coit Stadium and the Bears moving in. Having Ridgewood as a neighbor helped too, since the university brings over the college students.

Which is what brought me to town last year. I needed a change of scenery from Southern California, and decided to pursue my masters in education at Ridgewood U. I landed in Bridge Point simply for the slightly more affordable housing, then decided to do this semester fully online.

It's better that way, considering my new position with the Lane family.

Oh, God.

My mind floats back to the look on Declan's face.

Pressing my twin sister's name on my car's screen, the phone begins to ring obnoxiously loud through the speakers, assaulting my eardrums until she answers.

"Hey," Hartley greets me. Just hearing her voice sends calming frequencies through my body. I miss her so much.

Hartley and I are fraternal twins, although no one ever believes us because we're so different, both physically and in personality.

I groan at my sister dramatically. "My words didn't word properly again. I'm so embarrassed, Hart."

Her laughter fills the car. "Oh no, now what'd you say? And to who?"

"Who do you think?"

"You embarrassed yourself in front of your smokin' hot boss, didn't you?"

"Yup." I pop the p on purpose. "Start digging a hole."

"For your body or his?"

"Mine, because I've already died from humiliation. In fact, I'm speaking to you from beyond the grave."

Hartley exhales a laugh, and I can practically hear her eye roll. "Sorry. Can't. I love you too much, plus I'm not made for manual labor."

"Of course not. Much too lithe for that. How's rehearsals going?"

"No, no. Don't deflect," Hartley scolds. "What'd you say to your boss?"

"I made chocolate chip cookies, which he ended up baking for me because Sailor and I made a giant mess and I needed to get her cleaned up. But then, when I took them out of the oven, he joked and said something like 'you shouldn't be allowed to bake' and I said something like 'you haven't tasted my cookie yet.'"

There's a rustling behind the receiver, and as I slow for a red light, I white-knuckle my steering wheel, anticipating her response.

"What's so bad abou—oh. OH. *Hailey*!" Hartley's laughter fills the car so boisterously, I turn the volume down. She doesn't stop laughing until the light turns green and I'm about to turn into my neighborhood.

"You can stop laughing now."

"Only you could turn *that* into something more. Did he even put two and two together?"

"Of course he did. *Immediately*."

"What was his reaction?"

"Same as yours. I should quit, right? That's the only natural progression to this."

"You better not! You love working for him."

"*Loved*. Past tense. I loved working for him before I made an ass of myself." The repetitive click of my blinker competes against my words.

"Oh, stop. It'll all be blown over by tomorrow."

"When are you coming to see me?" I ask, putting my car in park. I leave it running, though, so I can finish talking to my sister. "I miss you, Hart."

"I know, I miss you too. I think the Rebels play the Bears here next month. Will you be flying down? Or are you stuck up in Bridge Point with the kiddo?"

"I'm coming down! There's going to be a few games, so Declan wants me and Sailor to come so he can still spend time with her when they're not on the field."

"I still can't believe you ended up with a nanny job for

the Bears coach. What are the odds we both end up connected to a baseball team in some capacity?"

"It's pretty funny considering dad's a football guy through and through."

"Now we're wearing jerseys for the wrong sports."

"Technically, you're the only one wearing a jersey. I'm wearing mac and cheese stains and flour on a T-shirt."

"Ew."

"Mmhmm. Alright, I just pulled into my driveway and need to go shower–I'm still covered in flour. I love you. Thanks for making me feel better."

"Always a phone call away."

"And a short plane ride," I singsong the end of our mantra to her. It's the only thing that got us through the first couple months being separated for the first time *ever*. "I'll see you next month."

When the call disconnects, I turn my car off and grab my purse from the passenger seat, watching my surroundings as I exit my car and head for the house. You can never be too careful.

When I'm inside, I don't bother turning the lights on and instead, drop my bag at my feet and schlep through the darkness up the stairs, ready to wash off the evidence of the day.

The mac and cheese.

Sailor's snot residue.

The flour.

And most importantly, the freaking embarrassment that's rooted into my mind.

And clothing.

All of it can wash down the drain with my jasmine and orange scented body wash.

Besides, tomorrow is a new day. Maybe Declan will forget all about my little word mishap by morning.

Maybe.

Hopefully.

CHAPTER TWO
Declan

Closing the door to Sailor's bedroom, I walk away quietly, hoping she stays asleep. Most nights, I wait until her breathing evens before slipping out into the hallway, but tonight I couldn't help but lie with her a little longer.

Her mother called me today.

Hearing from Addison always throws me in a tailspin if for no reason other than I can't stand the woman. I don't think I could ever fully hate her—she gave me the most precious part of my life—but I certainly don't respect her. She walked out when Sailor was just thirteen months old to pursue a career in acting, moving across the state to Hollywood without so much as a second thought for Sailor.

At the end of the day, though, it's Addison who's missing out. Which is why it's so important to me that Sailor is always surrounded by people who love and care about her. With a job as demanding as mine, finding the perfect nanny for our family was a feat similar to finding a needle in a haystack, but Hailey, so far, has been amazing.

It scares me how easily Sailor bonded with her. She's never been so comfortable around a nanny. Their fondness for each other was immediate, but that's more of a testament to Hailey's caring nature than my daughter's overly friendly one.

It also scares me how much my curiosity is piqued by the woman caring for my daughter. She's *exactly* my type, and I should have run for the hills after we met, but instead, I gritted my teeth and hired Hailey, knowing she was exactly what Sailor needed, too. She deserves the best, and I can push aside my physical attraction for the redheaded vixen, especially if it's in the best interest of the littlest love of my life.

When I make it back into my bedroom, I sink down onto the edge of my bed and drop my face in my hands, letting the tension of the day seep from my pores.

The Bears are going to be the death of me, or the cause of an early heart attack. With a roster of players younger than most in the majors, I feel like I'm the one babysitting these days. They're lucky they can play the hell out of a ballgame, or I'd be bitchin' to Blake, the team owner, about his approval skills.

Speaking of, my phone begins vibrating incessantly in my pocket again. With a deep groan, I swipe my hand down my face, stopping to rub my beard, then thrust my hips forward to pull my phone out.

My brows knit together as messages fly across the screen. I ignored this new group chat earlier, hoping it'd die before it began, but alas, the chat is alive, well, and blowing up my phone. Why I'm in a message with three of my players is beyond me, but with curiosity, I open it and begin to read.

AUSTIN COOPER

Ayy Coach. Dream team reporting for duty

GARETH FOX

What up. Who's in this one?

AUSTIN COOPER

Us, Fields, and Coach.

JENSEN FIELDS JR.

Great, another group chat. Stop making these, Cooper. Why not just make a giant team chat instead?

GARETH FOX

Do you actually want to talk to the whole team?

JENSEN FIELDS JR.

Not particularly.

AUSTIN COOPER NAMED THE CONVERSATION "COACH'S FAVORITES"

JENSEN FIELDS JR.

Seriously? That name makes us sound like we're children.

AUSTIN COOPER

Do you have a better name?

JENSEN FIELDS JR. NAMED THE CONVERSATION "THE BEARS"

AUSTIN COOPER

Snoozefest.

JENSEN FIELDS JR.

Better than coach's favorites.

GARETH FOX

Aren't we though?

JENSEN FIELDS JR.

Did you see his face earlier? He seemed pretty pissed when leaving.

GARETH FOX

Everyone played like shit, what do you expect?

JENSEN FIELDS JR.

Speak for yourself. I never play like shit even on my worst day.

AUSTIN COOPER

I was on my A-game.

GARETH FOX

Cocky much, Jensen?

JENSEN FIELDS JR.

For good reason, want to see it?

AUSTIN COOPER

Careful, your ego's showing.

GARETH FOX

It always is. That's why half the team hates him.

JENSEN FIELDS JR.

It's not my fault they all feel inferior to me.

GARETH FOX

Your holier-than-thou complex will be crushed if the rumors are true and Marsh gets traded to the Bears.

AUSTIN COOPER

Not only will that be funny as hell, but talk about some Nat Geo shit. FIELDS and MARSH on the BEARS. 🐻

AUSTIN COOPER

Why do you hate him again?

JENSEN FIELDS JR.

Because he's a piece of shit.

GARETH FOX

Childhood rivals, I think.

These three are making my head pound harder than it

has been, so I toss my phone onto my bed and strip down, opting to ignore the guys and rinse off my stress instead.

As the shower water heats up, I press my palms against the bathroom counter, letting my head hang, the weight of my life pressing against my shoulders. Steam rises from behind the shower curtain, and when my gaze hits the mirror, my reflection is hidden. Swiping the condensation with my palm, I stare at the man in the mirror and wonder how this life is *mine*.

Equal parts happiness and sadness consume me as I catalogue my appearance—the scruff of my beard that's quickly evolving from unkempt to mountain man. The length of my hair that *is* overgrown. The pools of dark collecting beneath my eyes.

I can't get a grip on my emotions as everything bull-dozes into me at once. The laughter I expelled earlier when Hailey made her unintended comment about her *cookie* opened the floodgates of everything I've been bottling up for the last year or so.

Right now, I feel like I could laugh and cry, and I haven't cried since I was a child.

Being a dad is hard.

Doing it on my own is harder.

Add coaching on top of that?

Some days it feels impossible.

But I am grateful, truly I am. Sailor and I are healthy. We have a beautiful house that I bought long before I met

Addison. My truck and car are paid off, and my bank account has more than I could ever need.

My cup is overflowing, yet in some aspects it's still empty.

I'm *lonely*.

So damn lonely, and I'm not sure I realized it until I watched the embarrassment bloom through Hailey's porcelain skin, and it dawned on me how much I miss laughing with someone. Making jokes. *Smiling*.

Having friends.

Pushing off the bathroom counter, I leave the shower running and walk buck ass naked into my bedroom and grab my discarded phone, pulling up the group message that's still going crazy. I need to make an effort with people again.

Austin, Gareth, and Jensen added me to their conversation, which means they're interested in being friends with me, right?

Why not give it a chance?

AUSTIN COOPER

I'm just saying, if I were Coach, I'd put Gareth as first batter over Kellen.

JENSEN FIELDS JR.

No one's disagreeing with you there.

GARETH FOX

I feel like I should be staying quiet
about this, but you know what? I
agree.

My fingers fly across the screen as I reply—
nothing long or drawn out, but enough to insert
myself.

No one said Kellen would be first up.

A text comes through immediately, and I'm surprised
to see Jensen has the fastest fingers.

JENSEN FIELDS JR.

Oh shit! Coach responded.

AUSTIN COOPER

COACH!

GARETH FOX

Now that you're here, do we have to
call you Coach, or can we call you
Declan?

AUSTIN COOPER

Or Deck?

Declan is fine, but on the field it's
Coach.

GARETH FOX

Noted.

AUSTIN COOPER

Heard.

GARETH FOX NAMED THE
CONVERSATION "THE FAVORITES"

An unfamiliar tug at the corner of my lips catches me by surprise as I look down at the phone, and I find myself actually grinning at the conversation.

I know they're just text messages, and these are my players, but having a lighthearted conversation feels good. It's something I've avoided in recent years, preferring to throw all my time and energy into Sailor and her needs, so much so that I've pushed aside mine.

It's startling how much I've lacked basic human contact outside of my workplace.

Sure, this is still technically an extension of work, but if I had to pick any guys from the team to become friends with, it'd be these three.

A lightness embraces me as I toss my phone back down and head back into the bathroom for that shower I promised myself almost ten minutes ago. Something in me shifted tonight, and I didn't realize I needed it until I walked in and saw an eruption of flour all over my kitchen.

This time, though, when I look at myself in the mirror, I don't scoff at my reflection. Somehow, in the last five minutes, it's felt like a page has turned in my book, and like I can finally relax into this next chapter.

And it all started because *she* made me laugh.

CHAPTER THREE
Declan

"Asses on the field in five!" Stalking through the locker room, I glare at the players as they change into their practice gear. They're wasting time by fucking around, pulling their practice uniforms on at a pace that could rival a snail.

I glance at my watch. Hailey's at the house for about three hours before she needs to head to Ridgewood for an on-campus exam. She's never expressed any sort of time restrictions when it comes to her availability, so I *really* want to make sure I respect this one request. Which means I need to wrap this practice up on time for once.

"Anyone who's not on the field at exactly ten will be benched," I bark, still striding through the room, trying to embody the authority I've been given.

A collection of groans echo through the space, along with some laughter. Pushing through the doors, they slam behind me as I make my way to the dugout. The metal bats clank when I toss my bag into the dirt.

Footsteps catch my attention, and I'm not surprised to find Jensen, Gareth, and Austin coming my way. A few of their other teammates linger by the side door leading from the field to the stadium.

"Hey, Coach." Gareth grins, then takes a long drink from his water.

Austin slaps me on the shoulder. "Glad you joined us in the group chat."

"I had a choice?"

Jensen grabs a batting helmet and pulls his favorite practice bat from the bag. "I tried to tell them you wouldn't engage, but you proved me wrong, old man."

"I'm *maybe* twelve years older than you." I glare at him, trying to remember if he's twenty-five or twenty-six.

"Makes a big difference in baseball." The bastard tosses me a wink then strides onto the field, swinging the bat as he walks.

Jensen Fields Jr. is arguably our best outfielder. He's incredibly quick and seems to have a sixth sense of where the ball is heading before it's even in the air. Not once have I seen him miss a catch unless it's in the stands.

"Don't let the grump bug you, Coach. His panties have been in a twist since he caught wind of Marsh's potential trade." Gareth suppresses a laugh as he tugs on a batting helmet.

Austin's behind him, shoving his hand into a mitt, listening intently.

Gareth is first batter and a wicked third baseman, while Austin's greatest strength is pitching. He's on his way to breaking records with that arm of his.

"Never said Marsh was coming over." I send a pointed look their way, my brows pinched. "Stop spreading shit."

Austin puts his palms outward in surrender. "Not me spreading rumors—" he tips his head at Gareth "—talk to Baby Face over there."

"It's not a rumor if you heard it from the mouth of the top dog." Gareth shrugs.

"Since when do you talk to Blake Bradley?"

"I don't." Gareth grins. "But that doesn't mean I don't hear things."

The rest of the Bears start filing into the dugout, so the topics of group chats, bad attitudes, and rumors are cut short.

For the next three hours, I dive into coach mode, directing drills, critiquing, and discussing potential plays. Around me, my assistant coaches all do their part with breaking the team into smaller groups and working with them in development, and focusing on areas for growth.

By the time I dismiss everyone, we're all sweating from the springtime sun, tired, and ready for lunch.

Austin surprises me with a rough clap on my shoulder.

"Any interest in grabbing a beer, Coach? We're heading to the pub after this."

"I thought we were going to Andromeda?" Gareth perks up from the dugout bench where he's kicking off his cleats in favor of his slides that he brought with him instead of leaving them in his damn locker like he's supposed to.

"Fuck no," Jensen chimes in. "Why would we drive all the way to Ridgewood to go to a biker bar?"

Gareth's shoulders deflate a little. "It's not just a biker bar," he grumbles, before turning his attention to a knot in one of his laces.

Austin shakes his head at Gareth, ignoring his sudden shift in mood, then turns back to me. "Anyway, beers?"

For a minute, while struggling with the zipper on my backpack, I consider it, before remembering two things. "It's one in the afternoon." Slinging my backpack over my shoulder, I shake my head. "And I can't. My nanny has somewhere to be today."

"Next time, then." Austin's expectant eyes widen a fraction. It's not a question, but a statement.

"Yeah, next time." My head nods in agreement, and the four of us walk across the field together.

"How old is your kid?" Gareth asks, peering around the guys.

"Sailor's three." For some reason, my answer feels

short, so I add, "You guys will meet her at the team barbecue next weekend."

"Awesome, man. My brother has a little boy around that age. Maybe I'll have them come and the kids can play."

"She'd love that. Sailor's a social butterfly."

"Great. I'll give my brother a call today and invite him."

Jensen adjusts his duffle bag, switching it to the other shoulder. "How's Cody's wife doing?"

Gareth shakes his head. "Not good."

The conversation drops, a heavy silence sinking amongst the men, and I'm left wondering what's wrong with Gareth's sister-in-law. I don't ask, though, because regardless of the situation, Gareth's obvious sorrow claws itself into my heart, too, and I think about the innocent child swept up in it all.

The moment Jensen pulls open the Bears' locker room door, the silence is flooded with chatter and the sound of running water from the players already in the shower.

I step inside, turning toward them and walking backward a few steps as they follow me in. "You guys have fun —and don't you dare drive drunk."

"Never," Austin promises. "Have a good weekend, Coach."

"See ya," Gareth says, and at the same time Jensen mumbles, "Later."

I walk away, shaking my head and suppressing a small smile.

I feel completely out of my depth here, but I have to admit, I like these guys.

"But I don't want her to go," Sailor cries as she fights against my hold, her tiny body thrashing in my arms as I struggle to keep her upright.

Crocodile tears stream down her face as she grabs my arm, looking over at Hailey with her bottom lip in a pout.

"I'll be back tomorrow, sweet girl." Hailey steps forward and places both hands on either side of Sailor's face. She's so close, her sweet scent of orange and florals fill my senses, and I stop breathing. Hailey tilts to kiss Sailor on top of her head, and I track the movement.

A pang of longing hits me square in the chest, and for a moment, I envision Hailey pressing up on her tiptoes to reach my lips next.

In the next second she steps back and gives me a small smile, and the vision is gone.

My vocal cords strain when I start to speak, so I clear my throat and try again. Vibration rumbles as I clear my throat. "Good luck on your exam."

Hailey's mossy eyes sparkle when our gazes collide. She

tucks a strand of her unruly red hair behind her ear. "Thanks."

Hand on the doorknob, she adjusts her purse strap on her shoulder and gives Sailor another warm smile. I see her hesitate as her gaze pulls from my daughter to me. With a tip of my head, I reassure her we'll be fine. Her lips tug upward again and she opens the door.

"Come back for dinner." The words rush out of my mouth faster than I can stop them—not in question, but in a command, which surprises...well, I think it surprises both of us, really.

Hailey's cheeks heat as her contemplative eyes search mine as she sinks her teeth into her bottom lip.

Thank God I'm still holding Sailor, because if it wasn't, I'm not sure I could stop myself from taking her face in my hands and crushing our mouths together.

What the fuck?

I need to get a grip—I cannot be attracted to Sailor's nanny.

"Are you sure?" Hailey questions. "I wouldn't want to impose."

I grunt. "Never an imposition. You'll be tired after your test. Might as well come back for a hot meal."

Hailey has been in our lives for the last two and a half months, and the only meals she's eaten with us have been meals she's cooked—which have been delicious, by the way. I'm not too shabby of a cook myself, and I'm even better with a smoker, which is why I add, "I'll throw the rib-eyes on the smoker. They'll be ready when you get back."

"That sounds great." She grins. "I'll see you both later then."

Setting Sailor down, I move to the front door and watch Hailey as she gracefully canters down the few steps of my porch and heads toward her car. She drives a gold sedan that looks like it's seen better days, and I have half a mind to offer for her to take my truck which is much safer, but that'd be overstepping. Definitely too much. If she was taking Sailor somewhere then sure, but she's not, so I shut my mouth and silently watch her go.

Hailey gives me a small wave as she pulls away from the curb, and I find myself lifting my hand in return, watching until her car is out of view.

Immediately I want her back in my sights, and that's not a fucking good thing.

As I go back inside, I realize how my house has dimmed without her presence. Even though she leaves and goes home every night, having her leave during the day feels like she's sucked the light and warmth from the bones of my house.

She's only gone to Ridgewood to take a damn test. She'll be back for dinner.

And even though Sailor's happily playing with her play

kitchen in the living room, she's quieter than she normally is when Hailey is home.

Home. What am I saying?

This isn't *her* home.

But it feels like it should *be?*

I don't know if I'm asking myself a rhetorical question or making a statement.

Dammit. I'm *so* fucked.

CHAPTER FOUR

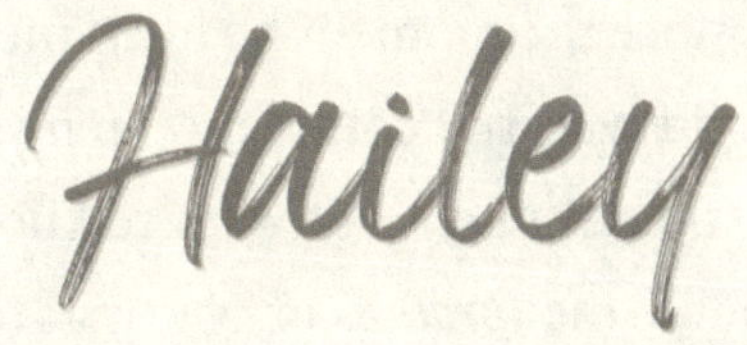

I've been sitting in my car in front of the Lane house for the last few minutes, giving myself a pep talk before going inside.

Throughout my entire exam, my thoughts strayed to Declan and his abrupt dinner invitation. It had come out of left field, baseball pun only *semi* intended, and even though I knew I *should* say no, I found myself saying *yes* instead.

There was something etched into Declan's expression that had me intrigued. Maybe it was the slight furrow of his brow, or the nervousness that flashed through his chestnut-colored irises. He looked like he was toeing the line between employer and *friend*, which is a title I'm not sure applies to us. We aren't friends... At least, I don't think we are. It made me wonder what was going on inside of that handsome head of his.

Throughout the duration of the exam, I had to keep trying to persuade myself that I said yes so easily because of Sailor, but deep down, I know I said it for myself.

My dumb ass is attracted to my boss, even though I've tried to deny it since the moment he hired me.

Even though I have full confidence in myself to remain professional, I still can't help but want to know him better. I fantasize about the *process* of getting to know him better... frequently.

Truth be told, Declan is a very busy man, and even though I work long hours in his home, our interactions have been minimal, reduced to a quick conversation after he comes through the door, or a series of short messages throughout the day with updates, or questions, regarding his daughter or the schedule.

Aside from the information I've gathered simply by being in his house, I really don't *know* him. But I want to —and therein lies the problem.

Because he's. My. Boss.

Blowing out a shaky breath, I push my car door open and step outside, admiring the late dusk sky. The sun slopes low on the horizon, its rays hardly visible as the last remaining hues of orange and pink fade into the inky backdrop of twinkling stars.

A shiver runs through me as I look up at the house. The season is changing—what was a comfortable warmth earlier in the day has transformed into a sharp crisp air that bites at the apples of my cheeks. Pulling my sweater tighter around my body, I take the stairs two at a time up the porch, and rap my knuckles against the door.

Anxiously, I chew on my bottom lip as I wait for Declan to answer, feeling a little awkward.

Maybe I should have declined.

I should have texted my sister.

A few seconds later, we're standing face-to-face, and a lopsided smirk pulls at his lips when he sees me. Pushing the door open further, he steps to the side for me to walk through. "Hey. Come on in."

"Thanks." My purse lands in its normal spot as I drop it to the floor once I'm inside.

"How was your test?" There's a soft click from the deadbolt engaging, then Declan turns to face me.

My eyes sweep over him, taking him in as if this is the first time I'm seeing him. In a way, it is the first time I'm seeing him like this—off the clock. With a dish towel slung over his shoulder, he's relaxed, wearing a gray T-shirt and dark wash jeans, with his feet bare.

The scent of garlic and rib-eyes waft in from the kitchen, and I lick my lips, although I might have done that because he looks so damn good right now.

Realizing my thoughts have run away with my libido, I try to hide the extended silence with a nonchalant shrug. "It was good, I'm pretty confident I passed."

"That's great." He tugs the dish towel from his

shoulder and spins it. "Make yourself comfortable—Sail's in her playroom if you want to say hi, but," he pauses, choosing his words carefully, "you're not here as her nanny, so don't feel like you have to work…" His voice lowers as he trails off. When our eyes idle, my pulse jumps in the hollow of my throat at the palpable tension between us.

I smile, shoving my hands into my pockets, suddenly feeling like I need to do something with them. "Everything smells amazing. Can I do anything to help?"

"Nope. Not at all. Dinner will be ready in about twenty, I'm just finishing up the potatoes." Declan winks. He. Freaking. Winks. And my panties incinerate. "Go take a load off."

Who is this man?

With another hearty grin, he stalks back into the kitchen, and I fear I might fall in love by the end of the night.

Or worse. Fall into his bed.

No. I won't let that happen.

He wouldn't let that happen.

There's a split second, though, where I feel a twinge of awkwardness not knowing if I should follow him and continue to make polite conversation, or head into Sailor's playroom to check on her.

As much as I want to follow after Declan, I know I

need to go say hi. Even the thought of being here without acknowledging her feels wrong—so I make my way down the hall, my steps slow as I take my time and lazily walk the path I hustle down so often.

The Lane house is stunning, and honestly, I'm understating its beauty with the term *house*. In my opinion, his home is what I'd call a mini mansion, and Declan has decorated it modestly, but in *very* good taste. It's no secret he has money, and while I don't know his net worth, I *do* know he earns a pretty penny as a coach, and that his family comes from old money.

I read somewhere that the Bears team owner went out of pocket to supply the team with better gear this year, including big salary bumps for *everyone*. Despite the Bears being under better ownership, it's also incredibly apparent they're in good hands with Declan as their coach too. Already the hype around the Bridge Point Bears has skyrocketed in comparison to last year.

Prior to taking the nanny job I did a little research on my boss and learned Declan's father owns a baseball team out in New York, and his grandfather was one of the most sought-after pitchers back in his day, and resides in the hall of fame.

The Lane family bleeds baseball.

When I turn the corner into Sailor's playroom, the familiar sound of her favorite Barbie movie plays in the background while she tinkers with a tea set at her small table. Leaning against the doorframe, I watch her and admire how well she navigates independent play, letting her imagination thrive.

After a few more seconds, she notices me and her face beams. Returning her smile, I cross the room and sink down onto my knees in the soft, plush carpet. "Hi, sweet girl. What are we playing? Tea party?"

Her little head nods enthusiastically, her soft brown ponytail wildly spinning. "Yes! Want some tea?" She holds out the floral plastic tea kettle.

"Why, that would be amazing!" I say in my most proper voice.

Sailor clanks the spout against the teacup and pretends to pour, then thrusts the cup into my face. "Here you go!"

"Oh gosh, this looks delicious." I bring the cup and hover it above my lips, making loud slurping sounds while pretending to drink. In true tea party fashion, my pinky is extended, too. Sailor mirrors my movements—down to the pinky, and together we drink our imaginary tea.

"This is the most delicious peppermint tea I've ever tasted, Sailor. Thank you."

"It's not peppermint. It's chocolate," she tells me, matter-of-factly.

"Oh? Chocolate, huh? I thought I tasted something a little bitter."

She wrinkles her nose, and I can't help but laugh. Reaching over I boop it with the tip of my finger.

Abruptly, she stands. "I'm hungry."

"Your dad's almost done cooking, I think. Should we go check on him and see if he's doing a better job in the kitchen than we do?"

She nods and reaches for my hand, and I let her pull me, making a show of standing up, pretending like it's *her* strength bringing me to my feet.

Together, we walk down the hall, crossing the bottom floor to the kitchen, where the aroma of savory scents is much, *much* stronger. As if on cue, there's a telltale rumble in my belly.

"Perfect timing, ladies." Declan moves a large pot from the stove to a hot pad on the counter, smiling at us as I help Sailor onto one of the stools at the island then take the one next to her.

"Can I do anything?"

"No, everything's good to go. Figured we could dish up buffet style." He tips his head toward the food set out in a line.

"Perfect. I'll dish Sailor." Sliding off my stool, I push hers in more. "Don't move, I don't want you to fall."

"What are you drinking? Beer? Soda? Sparkling water?"

"Sparkling water would be amazing, thanks."

As I pick up two plates—one for me, one for Sailor—Declan opens the fridge, glass bottles clanging together as he pulls out our drinks. Water for me, juice box for her, and a beer for him.

When we're settled around the informal dining table in the kitchen, I cut the tender smoked meat with my knife and it falls apart easily under the blade.

A moan floats past my lips when I taste it, unable to hold it in. It's indescribable and I close my eyes briefly as flavor explodes on my tongue with this first bite. "Holy shi—smokes," I catch myself. "This is amazing, Declan."

"Thanks. There's nothin' like throwing it on the smoker." His eyes light up as he watches me take another bite. "So, Hailey. I realized you've been helping me with Sailor for nearly three months now, and I barely know you. What do you do for fun?"

"Fun? With what time?" Snorting a laugh, I take another bite of my dinner, trying the potatoes. They're divine, and I practically moan in delight.

Across the table, Declan's face falls. "I know, I'm sorry my hours are so all over the place."

"Oh, no! That's not what I meant!" Guilt stabs me square in the chest. "I've been in college full-time since I graduated high school. There hasn't been much time for anything other than the college grind."

The moment his expression changes to relief, the coil in my chest relaxes, too.

"I like to read," I continue, shrugging, as I think about what else. "Spending time with family and friends before I moved away. Believe it or not, I'm actually a pretty good baker."

"Oh, I believe it. You made cookies, remember?" He smirks, and it sends a spark through my body that ignites instantly under his stare.

A little swoop in my belly tells me the playful glint in his eye is absolutely intentional, and he's remembering what I said last week.

Is he...flirting?

I think so.

It's been so long since a man flirted with me, that I take a long drink of my sparkling water, averting my eyes. It's easy to take the focus off him and shift my attention to Sailor, who chose the seat next to me. She's done well with everything on her plate, but I take the fork from her tiny hand and move everything into tight piles so it's easier for her to scoop her remaining bites.

I can *feel* Declan watching us, and without looking at him, I put the ball back in his court, my tone playful. "What do *you* like to do for fun?"

From my peripheral, he shifts in his seat, leaning back with his arms folded over his chest and a smirk on his face.

Once I'm done tending to his daughter, I sneak a glance.

"Well, these days I don't have much time for myself. If my focus isn't on the team, it's on Sailor."

"What about before adult life took over?"

"I played a lot of ball."

My nose scrunches at the clear-cut answer, and I quirk a brow, draping my arm over the back of Sailor's chair. My face must reflect my thought of wanting *more* of an answer than he just gave me. I want more of his flirtatiousness, in fact I'm craving it now, and I want to get to know *him*.

Declan sighs, rubbing his trimmed beard as he fights a smile. "Fine. you want to know what I really enjoy but haven't had the time lately to do?"

"Let me guess. Something criminal?" My voice is dry as I tease him.

"You caught me." He laughs, and I swear I feel the vibration of it deep in my core. I catch myself leaning forward, my elbow pressing against the table.

"My idea of a fun Saturday afternoon used to be volunteering at the local animal shelter."

For a brief moment I wonder if I heard him correctly. Immediately my mind conjures an image of Declan sitting cross-legged on the ground in front of a dog's kennel at the shelter, with cats and dogs smothering him with love. Inside I'm giddy and swooning over this man, but I can't make an ass out of myself in front of him again, so I force myself to remain cool as a cucumber. And on the exterior, I simply smile. "Do you like animals?"

The idiotic question rolls off my tongue before I can stop it. Clearly, my brain has stopped functioning. *Obviously, he likes animals, Hailey.*

"Not really, it was part of my court-ordered community service requirements." He smirks, teasing me as my cheeks grow pink. "I love animals. I just don't have time to own one."

"What's your favorite kind of animal?"

We sneak in bites of our dinner, engaging between content moments where we're simply eating.

"I'm a big dog person, the bigger the better. Although, there's something about a senior cat that's hard to resist. They used to be my favorite to visit at the shelter. On the outside they're grumpy, and standoffish, but gain their trust and they turn into complete puddles of purring mush."

"Stop! So sweet. You should adopt one, Declan. I'll help you take care of it."

"You'd do that?"

"Of course! Cats are pretty low maintenance, anyway. I wouldn't mind."

"I'll take that into consideration." Declan pauses, staring at me quietly. His eyes search mine so deeply, it seizes the breath from my lungs. Then, his next question wipes the smile right off my face. "So, what types of books do you read?"

How do I explain to him that my favorite type of

books are the ones where the heroine gets railed at least forty percent of the book—I'm talking filthy, explicit smut—and that shadow daddies make me wish men in books weren't fictional. I swear, all men—real life and otherwise—should be written by women. "Uhh, romance."

"You're blushing," he observes. His eyes narrow playfully as he props his elbow on the back of the chair, getting comfortable.

But I feel embarrassment creeping back in and I'm ready to hightail it out of here.

"Am I?" Nervous laughter bubbles up. "Anyway, thanks for the invitation to dinner. I was a little surprised."

"It was overdue," he rasps, his voice going gravelly as he drums his fingers against the table.

"Well, it's appreciated." I hold my fork with another bite up in the air near my mouth. "Your meat is delicious. Now I'm gonna want it all the time."

Oh, fuck my life, not again.

His eyebrow skyrockets up his forehead as my words resonate, but this time he doesn't laugh or crack a smile. Instead, he leans forward. "Maybe we can strike a deal then."

All the air squeezes from my lungs, and thundering doesn't even begin to describe what my heart is doing. It's morphed into a ping pong ball in my chest, and a sheen of sweat lines my forehead.

"Daddy, I'm all done," Sailor interrupts, but Declan keeps his attention focused on me.

"Okay, baby, go play."

Moments tick by slowly, the second hand on the clock on the wall seemingly the only noise in the room.

Sliding from her chair, Sailor skips out of the kitchen, leaving us alone.

The second she's out of earshot, Declan resumes. "Like I was saying. Maybe we can strike a deal. You do a lot around here. What if I prep the meat for meals, as time allows on the weekends, and you just handle the side dishes for a while?" He takes a bite, like he didn't just make me think this conversation was about to head in a completely different direction.

Despite the innocence of his suggestion, the underlying flirtatiousness—and alternate version my mind came up with—sends a zing of arousal straight to my core.

I swallow thickly, nodding. "That sounds like a deal."

I'm already doing all of the cooking—that was negotiated within my salary, knowing his hours would be unpredictable. It was important to him that Sailor didn't have leftovers every single night. And I really don't mind. A girl's gotta eat too.

"Great. So, what else should I know about you, Hailey?"

Well, for starters my pulse is through the roof because of you, sir.

"There's really not that much to tell, and I'm horrible at talking about myself. I'm much better with rapid fire questions."

He raises an eyebrow. "Play twenty questions?"

"Sure," I agree. "But only if I get to ask some, too."

"That's only fair. Favorite color?" His first question is so basic, I smirk.

"Easy. Yellow. You?"

"Red." His eyes drift to my hair, and my breath catches. "All-time favorite movie?"

I don't hesitate. "*The Wizard of Oz*. Favorite type of music?"

"Country, or rap."

Interesting. I smile, my pulse buzzing with delight. "Those are two very different genres."

"They both speak to the soul." There's a hint of a smile pulling at the corner of his lips. "What about you? Favorite type of music?"

"Whatever is on the radio," I quip.

"There's many different stations."

"You know! The mainstream stuff. Pop music."

Wrinkling his nose, he folds his arms over his chest and leans back in his chair. "Ah, a Swifty?"

I lift my shoulders in a playful shrug. "A little. Favorite breakfast food?"

"Bacon and eggs." He leans forward with his elbows on the table again, and having his sole focus on me spikes my nerves. *He's just so dang gorgeous.* "What's one of your bucket list items?"

"To stay in an over the water bungalow in Tahiti." There's no hesitation—it's my number one bucket list goal.

His eyes twinkle, looking mischievous for a moment. "That's a good one. I heard it's beautiful there."

"Do you travel often?"

"For the team, yes, but for pleasure? Not much."

"Well, you'll have to plan more family vacations." I laugh, even though my thoughts linger on the word *family.*

Where is Sailor's mom? I don't dare ask the question burning inside me.

Declan doesn't mirror my playfulness, and instead, I feel the shift in his demeanor as it shifts. He takes the last bite on his plate and stands abruptly, the back of his thighs pushing the chair behind him in a shrill scuff of wood against wood.

Grasping the neck of his beer bottle, he gives it a little shake. "You sure I can't offer you a better drink than water? I have a bottle of white zin in the fridge, too."

Game of twenty questions done, then, I guess. *Gotcha.* My teeth sink into my bottom lip. Do I want a drink? "I wouldn't want to overstay..."

He barks a laugh. "Sweetheart, at this point you live

here more than I do. Overstaying shouldn't even be a thought in your mind."

His words make my heart flutter, like a newly emerged monarch. Looking down at the nearly empty glass of sparkling water, I swirl what's left, barely carbonated.

My logical, professional side screams *bad idea*, the words flashing like a neon sign flickering with burnout, while my curious, lustful little hussy side is eager to spend more time with the hot single dad.

Bad.

Idea.

Still, I feel the grin as it radiates through my cheeks and I nod in agreement. "Yeah. A drink sounds great."

Maybe since I already ate the alcohol won't go to my head.

For a moment, Declan looks surprised I've said yes again, but then he stacks my plate onto his. "What'll it be?"

"I'll take a glass of wine if you don't mind opening the bottle."

"Not at all. I'd join you, but I'll stick to beer tonight." He saunters over to the sink, placing our dishes in before pouring my drink. When he hands me the stemless wine glass, our fingers brush, and for a moment it's like time stops.

That seems to happen a lot when he's around.

For a second, I forget how to breathe.

Our lingering stare shatters when Sailor appears at my side, holding Snug-Bug as she audibly yawns.

Wrapping my arms around Sailor's small waist, I lift her to my lap, both for my own distraction and because she's swaying slightly. "Tired?" She immediately leans into my chest, nodding against it.

The clock shows it's after seven, which is still a little early for bedtime, but she had a big day with lots of sun and fresh air. In the morning we ran errands and played at the park, and I'm sure she was playing in the backyard while I was gone.

"I'll take you upstairs after I put the food away, Sail." Declan's husky voice pulls my attention back to him like a magnet.

"I can get her ready for bed." With Sailor in my arms, I stand, adjusting her into an easier hold. She wraps around me like a spider monkey, resting her head on my shoulder as her thumb slips into her mouth. I don't have to look to know her eyes are already closed.

"You don't have to, you're not—"

"I *want* to do her routine with her, Declan. I got this, don't stress." And I mean it. It took half a second for me to fall in love with Sailor. If he asked me to, I'd probably agree to work for free, just to help him out. I *care*. Probably more than I should considering I'm just temporary in their lives.

At any point Declan could meet someone who falls

perfectly into the role of *stepmom*, or maybe Sailor's *actual* mom could come back into the picture.

Both thoughts make my stomach roil with every step I take, climbing the stairs to the second story.

As I reach the landing, an image as clear as a snapshot flashes through my mind of Declan and I, each holding one of Sailor's hands as we walk through a park, letting her swing between us while we lift her higher. It's the epitome of a candid family portrait, and is as jarring as it is exhilarating.

How did I go from staying for a drink to these wild thoughts?

You need to get laid, Hailey, my sister's voice rings through my ears. It's exactly what she'd say if I were to call her right now. She'd laugh and chastise me, insisting that my wayward imagination is my fault because I'm the one who saw how gorgeous Declan Lane was and still took the job.

Just because someone is attractive doesn't mean anything, right? I've been good and kept my thoughts, and *hands*, to myself.

Plus, he doesn't even like me. The newfound flirting is a fluke. A one-off.

Just like the vision my mind just conjoined as I stare at the empty tub, of a smaller toddler splashing with Sailor as I get them *both* clean and ready for bed.

Shaking my head, I snap myself out of lala-land and focus on caring for Sailor.

That's what I need to do right now. Not fall down this rabbit hole of delusion.

Picturing a whole ass life with the man I nanny for was *not* on my bingo card this year. But now, as I draw Sailor a bath filled with her favorite bubbles and her Scuba Barbie, more flashes of what could be overtake my thoughts.

And I... I think I like what I see.

CHAPTER FIVE

Declan

The reoccurring playlist of the different sounds Hailey makes has been on a constant loop through my mind. I replay her laughter, her gasps, and even the way she snorts a boisterous laugh when she finds something hilarious.

There's been no reprieve from the visions of the stunning redhead who has become a part of my daily life.

I long to squeeze her curves, feel her supple skin in my hands, rake my teeth against her breasts. *Taste* her.

If I could only be so fucking lucky.

All week I've had to remind myself she's here for two reasons—Sailor and a paycheck. Although she stated otherwise last week when she stayed for dinner, making it perfectly clear how she feels about Sailor.

"I want to put her to bed..."

What do you want with *me* then, sweetheart? Seems

like we've strayed past the line of employer-employee, and are treading lightly in the friend zone.

And a friend is all Hailey Shea can ever be. My nanny is off-limits, no matter how bad I want to taste her, touch her, and *feel* her.

Speaking of my dick, this is the third morning in a row I've woken up painfully hard. Clearly *he* didn't get the memo about not crossing any lines.

Lazily, I look at the alarm clock and realize I've hit snooze too many times and now I'm running late. Hailey's likely already downstairs getting Sailor fed.

"Ugh," I scoff, tossing my comforter to the side before I swing upright, my bare feet hitting the cold flooring. Palming my aching shaft, I adjust myself in my pajama bottoms, heading to my en suite.

Peppermint assaults my mouth, counteracting the inevitable morning breath, as I brush my teeth, but by the time I finish, my morning wood hasn't calmed the fuck down.

Glancing at myself in the mirror, my jaw clenches as I tell myself to stop acting like a teenager and ignore my hard-on.

Then my thoughts drift back to Hailey and I'm a goner.

Flipping the lock on the bathroom door, I stalk back to the sink and stare at my reflection again for a moment, silently chastising myself for letting my fantasy run rampant.

Then I push down my pants.

My dick springs free, thick and engorged, and I waste no time wrapping my palm around it, stroking the way I've done countless times.

Only unlike the times before, a certain redhead flashes through my mind as I pump from root to tip.

This is so wrong.

"*Fuck*," I moan. Why does wrong feel so damn good?

Releasing my dick, I spit into my open palm, then grip my shaft tighter.

Bracing myself with one hand against the bathroom counter, my hips thrust in time with my strokes, and I tip my head back in pure blissful agony.

With each charge forward, I inch closer to my release. I fuck my hand with fervor, my mind never straying from Hailey. I picture her smile, and the way her lips would look so pretty wrapped around me.

Would she take me down her throat, letting me fuck her face until she swallowed every last drop? Or would she prefer to be in charge, guiding me to my release with precise flicks of her tongue against—

My balls tighten, and that's the only warning I have before I detonate, coming so hard my hand slaps against the counter and I groan long and hard as my cum shoots like a geyser against the lower cabinets.

My body hums in relief as I expel days of pent-up

tension, the evidence now pooling on the floor. But I give myself a minute, my eyes closing as my chest rises and falls while I come down from heaven.

Fifteen minutes later I'm dressed and ready for the day, the bathroom cleaner than it was. I push away the guilt about *who* was on my mind while I chased my release, though I'm not claiming to be a perfect man.

The glaring fact of the matter is I'm insanely attracted to Hailey. I can't deny that she's beautiful, nor should I have to. But I absolutely, under no circumstances, will fuck this up for Sailor. So I remind myself *again*, for the third time in five minutes, that she's off-limits. That includes fantasizing about her.

What I just did in the bathroom—it's a one-off.

It has to be.

As I descend the stairs, Hailey's laughter—her genuine, pure elatement—echoes through my under-furnished home. The sound makes me freeze mid-step as it pierces me through the chest, immediately bringing a smile to my face.

When I round the corner, two sets of eyes snap at me. "Morning ladies." I stop in front of Sailor, bending to press a kiss against the top of her head. "How's everyone doing today?"

"Hailey made pancakes!" Sailor's excitement carries through her voice, then she stuffs her mouth full of another bite of the syrup-doused pancake.

"I see that, they smell delicious."

"Can I make you a plate?" Hailey moves around the counter and reaches for a clean dish for me before I can answer.

"I'm running late, but thank you. I'm just going to grab a protein shake." *Although, the only thing I'm hungry for, sweetheart, is you.*

Walking around the opposite side of the counter, I reach into the top cabinet to grab a shaker bottle.

When I turn to grab some almond milk from the fridge, I don't realize Hailey is standing so close, and my chest bumps into her shoulder. "Shit. Sorry!"

"I'm sorry!" she says at the same time, her cheeks growing rosy. "Let me make you a to-go box, that way if you're hungry later, you'll have something." Hailey side-steps and reaches into a different cabinet to grab a glass container. "I cut up some strawberries earlier, too."

"You're too good to us."

She smiles, then seconds later we both reach for the refrigerator, and my hand covers hers as we both try to pull it open.

My skin against hers is electrifying, and I'm taken

aback by the intense urge to tangle our fingers together just so I can make the feeling last longer.

"Oh my gosh! I'm sorry!" She giggles. Stepping away from the fridge quickly, she turns to the kitchen island, and I close it. Without meaning to, my eyes trail her body, hugged perfectly by a light yellow shirt with flowers on it and tight jeans.

"All good." I let out a strained chuckle, turning my attention elsewhere. The physical contact *and* the view made my dick hard and now I'm thinking about her thighs wrapped around my head. *Fuck*. "On Saturday we're having our team barbecue at the stadium at three. I'd love for Sailor to be there." *And you.* "Think you could bring her for a bit?"

"Of course! Happy to."

"Thanks." What am I supposed to be doing right now? *Oh, right. Protein shake.*

Never grabbed the almond milk.

It's a weird feeling—hard for me to tell what type of tension it is, at least from her.

Mine is pure, carnal need for this woman and I can't explain why, all of a sudden, I'm feeling *desperate* for her.

Clearing my throat, I pull the stainless steel door open again. "Should be back early tonight. Hopefully."

There's a soft sound of a container lid hitting the counter as I pull out the half-gallon carton, letting the fridge slam once I'm out of the way.

With a rapid turn I take a step forward and immediately crash into Hailey, who's bent over at the waist. As my semi-hard groin connects with her incredible ass, our bodies seem to fuse together like magnets. Hailey sucks in a sharp breath at the contact and on instinct, my free hand flies to her hip, gripping it tightly as she straightens.

For several long, torturous but incredible seconds, neither of us moves, and as subtly as possible, I breathe her in.

Wrong move, because it sends my dick into a full salute. With my shaft now completely poking into her in greeting, I'm forced to step back. Again, I clear my throat. "I'm so sorry."

Emphasis on the so. *Please don't sue me for harassment I'm just so damn attracted to you I can't fucking think straight.*

The look on her face can only be described as horrified as her round, emerald eyes widen. "What? You are?"

Shit. I said that out loud.

Fuck it.

I smirk at her, but don't touch on the subject further. "I've got to run."

Flee, more like.

Abandoning the almond milk and shaker bottle on the counter, I rush to Sailor and give her another quick kiss on top of the head. "Love you, Sail. Daddy will see you in a few hours, okay?"

I vaguely register my daughter saying goodbye as I practically sprint from my kitchen, unable to look Hailey in the eye.

She's going to quit. I practically dry humped her from behind in the middle of my kitchen, after jacking off to the thought of her this morning. Thank *fuck* she doesn't know the latter, or I'd probably be in cuffs by now.

By the time I make it out of my driveway and onto the road, my heart is racing and I'm still hard from remembering how Hailey's body felt against mine. I'm fucked, so fucked.

I want her.

God dammit, she's the last person on this planet I should want.

Resting my hand on top of the steering wheel I coast down the freeway and palm my aching shaft that will not calm the fuck down, trying to adjust quickly—the stadium is about to come in to view.

The last thing on my mind should be the redheaded vixen caring for my daughter, spending her days at my home and already fitting in so perfectly to our lives.

I should be thinking about work. About the Bears.

My to-do list for today is so long, I'm not sure I'll accomplish everything—not with the way these dickheads on the team act with each other. It didn't take long for them to settle in as a family, taunting and pranking each other at every turn, which I do appreciate. Makes my job slightly easier.

But I know I'll have my work cut out for me today when I see Jensen, Austin, and Gareth leaning against a brand new, blacked out, McLaren Artura the second I pull into the nearly empty stadium lot. I don't know which one of these dumbasses mismanaged their money this immensely, but I swear twenty-somethings shouldn't have access to the millions they earn each year.

Gareth's smile broadens as I pull up next to the car. I'd put money on it being Austin's. Seems like something he'd go out and buy.

"Hey, Coach." Gareth pops open the top of a pink donut box, presenting it to me as I hop out of my truck.

"Mornin'," I grumble, purposely leaving out 'good' since it hasn't been that great on my end. My brows furrow. I can't believe I fucking did that.

"Thought we could all use something sweet this morning."

Grabbing my duffle from the backseat, I eye the donuts while I nudge both car doors closed. The box would send my kid into a frenzy. Cake donuts with frosting of chocolate, vanilla, strawberry, and—

"Sprinkles?"

"Fuck ya." Austin grabs a pink one and shoves half into his mouth. "These are the best. Don't try to deny it." Crumbs fly from his lips with every syllable.

Gareth shakes his head at Austin. "For some reason this is the only thing the donut shop had left."

"You're a fucking pig," Jensen scoffs, his face full of disgust as he looks at Austin.

Austin simply laughs. "Oh, c'mon. Pull the stick out of your ass, Fields."

"I'm good, thanks though," I finally say to Gareth once the exchange between Jensen and Austin is over. He closes the lid.

"I expect you three on the field in ten." I press the key fob in my pocket, engaging the lock on my truck.

"You got it!" Austin calls out, but I'm already a quarter of the way through the parking lot.

I was right—I'm going to have my work cut out for me today.

Hailey

By the time I hear Declan's keys clinking together as he unlocks his front door, I'm curled up on his couch under a blanket, with a bowl of popcorn in my lap and one of my favorite movies playing.

It's another late Friday night spent at the Lane house, but honestly, I don't mind. I knew exactly what I was getting into when I took the job, and I'd rather be here than in my outdated condo alone. Their house has become familiar to me in a way I never imagined it would.

My fingers know exactly where each and every light switch is without thought. My belongings, such as my purse, and my shoes, have designated spots. I find myself positioning my shoes next to Declan's in the entryway. It's both terrifying and comforting to say their house has become my home away from home.

Now, Sailor's fast asleep, and I went into a bit of a

cleaning frenzy earlier, after turning in the last of my weekly coursework and discussions.

"Hey," Declan greets when he makes it inside, quietly shutting the door behind him. The glow from the paused movie illuminates his features as he gives it a glance, no doubt trying to see what I'm watching.

A shiver runs through me from the timbre of his voice, and I'm captivated for a moment before I remind myself to speak, not just stare. "Hey. How was your day?"

Without turning the lights on, he drops his bag, and in a few strides, sinks onto the plush cushion beside me. He stretches his legs out in front of him, and wastes no time scooping up a handful of popcorn. The move feels so intimate, like we're a couple who's been together for years.

"Long. Sailor good today?" he asks before popping some of the salty snack into his mouth.

Pinching the soft fleece of the blanket, I roll it around between my fingers, avoiding Declan's gaze. "She's always good."

The way my heart is beating, I fear it might actually explode. I don't need to look up to feel his eyes on me. And I don't need his hands on me to remember the searing heat of his touch.

It's borderline pathetic how much I've thought about him since that encounter in the kitchen a couple days ago.

But I can't help it. I want to feel him again. I want

more of his hands on me, caressing my skin in a way that makes me tremble. I want to feel him *everywhere*.

With Declan's eyes trained on me, his voice vibrates with intensity when he says, "Because she loves you."

My skin pebbles with goosebumps. There's something in his tone that makes me wonder if... No, maybe I just want there to be.

"I'm very lucky my landlord connected us. I love watching Sailor."

And I mean that with my entire heart. That little girl has me wrapped around her finger.

With the same deep timbre that drew me and sent a shiver through me a second ago, Declan says, "You both deserve the world."

Butterflies explode in my stomach. I'm at a loss for words that I'm willing to speak aloud. My eyes drop to his lips and I find myself wanting to toss the popcorn bowl to the ground and crawl into his lap. I can't help but wonder if he'd let me.

It's hard to know.

Declan glances at the TV again, pulling me from my errant thoughts. "I'm going to go shower. Feel free to hang out until your movie's done."

With a simple sentence it feels like he just took a Sharpie to reinforce that hypothetical line.

Time for me to leave. "Oh that's okay!" I say as nonchalantly as possible, trying to keep my emotions out of my already shaky voice. Declan pushes to his feet, and I move the popcorn bowl while unfolding my legs from the pretzel they're in. "I just started it. No big deal."

My heart beats erratically with the need to flee even though he literally *just* told me to stay because if he wanted me here, wouldn't he stay and watch it with me?

As I lift my blanket, Declan puts his hand over mine, stopping it midway. His touch freezes me, and the look in his deep brown eyes is gentle as he says, "Stay. Watch your movie. I'll be right back."

A light squeeze on my hand has me sucking in a sharp breath before he releases it and reaches for the remote. With the click of a button, he brings the movie back to life and tosses it onto the spot he occupied on the couch.

Then, without another look in my direction, he heads toward the stairs.

The air whooshes out of me the moment he's out of view. Trembling, I try to focus on the actors on the screen, but for the next twenty minutes the only thing I can think of is the man upstairs, naked in the shower.

His words.

Those looks he gives.

His touch.

It feels like something is shifting between us, and I'm more confused than ever. Surely, this is all in my head. I've seen a picture of Sailor's mom. I'm *nothing* like her.

We're opposites in every way.

The next several minutes are spent gaslighting myself and overthinking every word the man has ever spoken to me. When Declan returns, I couldn't tell you what's happening in the movie I've seen so many times prior.

The scent of his body wash envelops me—cedarwood mixed with a light citrus and bergamot—and when he sits, it's closer than he was before. The cushion-length gap between us is gone, and we're side by side. Immediately, heat rushes to my core.

"So, what movie is this?" Declan asks, casually draping his arm over the back of the couch, his hand parallel with where my head would rest if I laid it back.

"*Crazy Stupid Love*." I'm hyper aware of his proximity—I can practically feel his skin.

"Never seen it."

Clearing my throat, I shift in my seat a little, which does nothing to help the situation—now my knee is touching his leg. My pulse quickens, that simple touch electrifying through my body. "It's cute. It's about a guy whose wife blindsides him by asking for a divorce, then a guy he meets at a bar decides to help him try to be more attractive to women, but he's a womanizer and ends up dating the other guy's daughter. I'm not explaining it well."

"Sounds like a chick flick." Declan gives me a coy smile.

"Kind of. Romantic comedy for sure."

"Cool."

Cool? How do I keep this conversation going?

"Cool." I nod like a dumbass.

And now the conversation's killed.

A silence settles over us and eventually, my nerves calm and I find myself getting cozier on the couch. Declan laughs at all my favorite parts, and I sneak glances at him whenever I'm positive he's not paying attention.

Eventually though, I fall asleep. When I wake, the glow from the TV is gone, and the room is eclipsed with inky darkness from the wee hours of the night. Using the flashlight on my phone, I try to regain my bearings and notice Declan asleep on the couch next to me.

He looks serene with his hair draped over his forehead, his arms folded over his chest as he quietly sleeps.

Slipping off the couch, I tiptoe across the room and slip my feet into my sandals, while picking up my purse at the same time, not making a sound as I do.

"You don't have to leave." Declan's voice is gruff, thick with sleep as he sits up and yawns. "Guest room's all yours if you want."

God, how I want to say yes to that. But I know I shouldn't.

"Thanks, but I don't have anything with me for tomorrow. I'll be back in the morning."

"You sure?" He's groggy as he crosses the room to

meet me at the door. "This is a shit time to be out. The bars just closed and the drunk drivers—"

"I'll be okay, I promise." I *have* to go home. I can't explain why—no, actually I can. It's because of the way he's looking at me that I say no. Like he's worried—like he wants me here. My heart can't take it, and I'm about to kiss him. I *can't* let that happen. Taking a step back to create some distance between us, my hand grips the doorknob behind me. "Goodnight, Declan."

Licking my lips, I take another step back but don't miss the way his eyes drop for a brief second before they connect with my face again.

His throat bobs. "Goodnight, Hailey."

Stepping out into the crisp, darkened night, I hurry to my car and don't bother letting it warm up before I put it into drive. The entire way home, my thoughts are consumed with one thing only.

Him.

CHAPTER SEVEN

Declan

"Hi! I'm here! Sorry!" Hailey blazes through the door in a whirlwind, dropping her purse in its normal spot.

I love that she has "normal spots" for the things she brings into my home, and that she's become so comfortable here.

Seeing her stirs something in my chest. I've been replaying last night over and over in my mind, and goddamn did I want to kiss her so many times.

It was entirely too easy to picture myself pulling the elastic from her hair and watching her waves of copper tumble down from where she had it piled on top of her head. I fantasized about tilting her head back as we consumed each other in a kiss that left us both wanting more.

But then the moment passed, and we refocused on the

chick flick she had on, before accidentally passing out on the couch for a couple hours.

I was exhausted.

Which is why, against my better judgment, I let her drive home alone at two-thirty in the morning, when I should have thrown her over my shoulder and deposited her in the spare bedroom.

I almost texted her to make sure she made it back safely. I typed out two different messages and deleted them both.

But I'm still not sure where her head is at. She looks at me like she wants me, but if I cross that line with her and I'm wrong? Not only would I have completely misread everything, but I'd be screwing up an important relationship for Sailor.

And if there's one thing my daughter needs in her life it's a strong female presence.

Sailor loves Hailey more than I've ever seen her love another adult besides me. The last thing I want is to risk their bond for something that may never work.

But it's getting increasingly hard to ignore the feelings I have for Hailey. She's more than just someone I'm attracted to, despite trying to convince myself that's all it is. She's everything I didn't know I wanted until I laid eyes on her.

And she's the one person I can't fucking have.

It's especially difficult to pretend like I don't want to

taste every inch of her skin when she breezes into my home looking as good as she does, like a walking temptation with crimson cheeks that match her hair.

To stop myself from grinning like a fool, I look down at the meat I'm preparing for the team barbecue.

"Don't sweat it," I reply coolly, ignoring the immediate reaction my body has to her presence.

Ripping another long piece of aluminum foil, I place it over the extra-large disposable roasting pan full of marinated chicken, squeezing along the edges to seal it. "I'm running a little behind today, too."

"What can I do to help?" She doesn't hesitate in her offer and goes straight to the sink to wash her hands.

I rip another piece of foil for the last roasting pan. "Nothing, I'm just about done."

A bang to my right draws my attention, Sailor's legs are swinging against her chair as she sits and colors, singing a song that I recognize from one of her cartoons. She's so engrossed in what she's coloring, she hasn't even looked up to spot Hailey yet.

"What time do you want us there?" The water shuts off, and she dries her hands on a paper towel before throwing it away.

My breathing stalls as she leans against the counter next to me, running her hand through her hair. With her full attention on me, I forget how to speak.

God, she's beautiful.

My eyes drop to her lips, but I don't let them linger. "You're welcome whenever. It starts at three, and food will be ready a little after."

"Sounds good, we'll be there!" Her smile sends a spike of exhilaration through my chest. Crossing the room, she goes over to Sailor and switches gears into nanny mode.

I stop what I'm doing to watch her with my daughter for a moment, and I'm caught off guard when seeing her being so attentive and maternal ignites something in me that I've never experienced until this exact second. I'm so unprepared for the onslaught of emotions, I have to set my hand on the counter to ground myself. Every fiber of my being screams to walk over, pick her up, and take her upstairs to make her mine.

I've seen her interact with Sailor countless times, but now I'm envisioning *more*.

I'm brought back to this fucking dimension when Sailor hops to her feet, abandoning her crayons, and pads over to where I stand, shoving her coloring page at me. "Daddy! Look at my unicorn picture."

My chest rises and falls in rapid succession as I drag my eyes from Hailey and I take the drawing from Sailor, looking down at the thick black outline of a cartoon unicorn. "Wow, Sail, how pretty. Should we hang it on the fridge?"

Her head bobs in agreement and she races over to the

refrigerator, grabs an alphabet magnet, and thrusts it at me with her chubby hand.

Despite being three, she hasn't lost the dimples in her knuckles. It makes me nostalgic for the early days when she was an infant and would stare up at me with her big, blue eyes.

Together we find a spot for her art, and once it's hung, she steps back with her hands bracketing her hips as she admires it.

Kneeling, I plant a kiss on her cheek. "Hailey will bring you to Daddy's work later, okay? Be good."

She nods, then wraps her arms around my neck in a hug. "Okay! Bye, Daddy!"

Easily distracted, she runs off to the playroom, disappearing from sight, and leaves me alone with Hailey. A calm silence settles around us as we both stare in the direction she went.

After a second, I snap out of it and pat my pockets, making sure I have my wallet and keys. I do, so I lift up the roasting pans, glancing at the clock on the stove to see how late I am.

Yeah, I need to get on the road. "See you in a few hours. If you need anything, give me a call."

"Likewise," Hailey chirps. "If you forget anything, let me know and I'll bring it."

My brain stops sending signals to my body at the sight

of the most beautiful smile Hailey flashes me, halting me dead in my tracks.

Every drop of blood in my body races to my dick, and right now, I'm grateful to be standing behind the kitchen island. I have to clear my throat before I answer, "Thanks."

Lucky for me, and the hard-on I'm now sporting, Hailey doesn't linger. Instead, she gives me a small wave and leaves in the direction Sailor went.

Things would have gotten awkward if I had to wait behind the counter for my dick to chill the fuck out after we'd just finished saying goodbye.

But now I find that I *am* lingering, staring past the kitchen instead of getting my ass on the road.

When I arrive at the stadium, most of the team, and their friends and family are there, congregated on the baseball diamond. Barbecues have been brought in and are set up near the dugout. Everywhere I look, people are laughing and having a good time already. Some are setting up extra tables and chairs, while others are shooting the shit in small groups, or tossing a ball back and forth in the outfield.

A spark of pride blooms in my chest.

One of my fears with becoming head coach was that I'd struggle to maintain that sense of family and familiarity amongst the team—feared they'd view me as *the new guy*.

But this might be the best turnout we've had at a barbecue in years.

With a grin on my face, I head straight for an empty table and set down the pans of meat, nodding at a couple of the guys in greeting as I pass by.

"Ay, Coach is here," Austin's voice rings out from behind me, and when I turn, his hand's already outstretched, ready for me to shake.

Gareth and two other men trail behind, beer bottles in hand, laughing as they come to join us. One has similar features to Gareth but appears to be a couple years older, although not by much despite the salt and pepper sprinkled throughout his chestnut hair. The other guy is the definition of a California boy, with unruly, shoulder length blond hair, and bright blue eyes.

"Hey, Coach. I want you to meet my brother, Cody," Gareth introduces us, and Cody outstretches his hand, which I take in a firm handshake.

"Hey Cody, nice to meet you."

"He's the one with a kid around your daughter's age. And this is Dylan," Gareth continues, not letting his brother get a word out. "Dylan and I have been friends since we were in grade school."

"Nice to meet you." I tip my head in a greeting. Austin reappears with a beer in hand, and takes a bottle opener from his pocket to crack it open for me.

The bottle is cold to the touch, moisture beading against the rich amber glass, and I take a nice long pull of the crisp drink.

"Great to finally meet the man who has to deal with this guy day in and day out." Cody tosses his arm around Gareth's shoulder, dragging his brother into a playful embrace.

"Hey, I'm the least of Coach's worries."

Chuckling, I pivot the conversation. "Gareth mentioned you'd bring your son? I have a daughter who's the same age." There's a few children running around. I guess I could have brought Sailor with me and given Hailey the afternoon off.

"Yeah, Bodhi is over there running around." Cody tips his head toward a boy who's racing toward the outfield, waiting for the other kids to chase him.

"My daughter Sailor's nanny will bring her in a few hours."

"Oh, he'll *love* that. Bodhi always makes it his personal mission to befriend every child everywhere we go."

Gareth's friend Dylan laughs. "You mean he befriends the little girls everywhere he goes?" He nudges Cody. "You'll have to watch that one when he's older."

I quirk a brow in silent question as the three men in front of me laugh at their inside joke, but I don't ask them to elaborate.

"It's nice that you have a nanny. Could use that from time to time," Cody muses, and my memory flickers back to when Gareth told me Cody's wife is sick.

"Hailey is a lifesaver. I'm grateful to have her." Taking

another pull of my beer, I shift my focus to the rest of the attendees and scope everyone out. Cody doesn't say anything further, and for a brief second I feel like I should offer to ask if Hailey would ever want to babysit before I think better of it. It's not my job to offer up her services—not to mention, I employ her full-time.

"So, Coach. Do you live in Bridge Point?" Dylan asks, clapping me on the back. He's wearing light blue shorts with Hawaiian flowers, a plain white T-shirt, and brown leather flip-flops, leaning into the laid-back persona I'm stereotyping him to have.

"You can call me Declan. And yeah, Bridge Point's my hometown. We moved a few times when I was a kid but always ended up back here. You?"

"Ridgewood." He grins. "Born and raised, but I moved down to San Diego after high school."

"What brought you back?" I let another swig of beer sit on my tongue for a moment before swallowing the crisp, bitter taste down.

His face drops for a fraction of a second before he smiles tightly. From my peripheral, I see Gareth switch his weight from one foot to the other, as though he's anticipating Dylan's next words. "My mom passed away, and our dad lives across the country. My little sister never left Ridgewood, so I moved back to be near her."

"Bro, your sister is only a year younger than you." Gareth's eyes narrow for a beat.

"Yeah," Dylan says sarcastically. "*Little* sister."

Gareth shakes his head and takes another drink.

I look between Gareth and his best friend, trying to figure out what the sudden shift in attitude is, before saying, "Well, you and your sister will have to come to a game sometime."

Dylan beams. "Yeah! Indy would love that. If we can get her to take a night off from the bar, that is."

Gareth mumbles something under his breath then takes a long drink before tossing the bottle into a trash can. He shakes his head and walks over to join Jensen a couple of tables over.

"She's a bartender?" I ask politely, although I'm looking for an exit strategy.

"Yeah, at a biker bar in Ridgewood called Andromeda."

"That's cool."

"Ever been there?" he asks curiously.

"Can't say that I have."

"We should all go sometime." Dylan grins and pulls his phone from his pocket. Without looking back up at me, he adds, "Betcha we could get a round on the house."

"Yeah, maybe after a home game sometime," I tell him to placate him, but I have no intention of ever going to a *biker* bar with a man who looks like one of Sailor's Ken dolls. Even if it is with a group.

Excusing myself from the conversation, I walk over

and fire up the barbecue so I can get started on cooking. Everyone seems content for now, but I've been at enough of these things to know there's a fine line between having a good time and being irritated that there's no food.

It seems like the blink of an eye by the time I'm standing around the hot charcoal flipping the last few pieces of chicken. I've spent the better part of my time at the grill chatting with the three men who've made it their mission to befriend me, and when Sailor finally arrives and flings herself at my legs, she holds me in a tight hug and says, "Hi, Daddy!"

"Hey, baby girl." I pick her up, situating her on my hip like I've done so many times prior.

"Damn," Austin mutters under his breath and I glance up to see Hailey walking through the gathering with a million-dollar smile on her face. Or at least that's how much I'd pay just to catch a glimpse of it.

A swell of possessiveness inflates within me at Austin's outward appreciation, but I can't rip my gaze from her long enough to give a shit if he's staring.

Hailey lights up the stadium as she keeps her sole focus on Sailor and I, unknowingly ignoring everyone who's stopped mid-conversation to look at her.

She's a vision, and she has no fucking idea.

"Hey," she greets, stopping on the other side of the grill. A plume of smoke wafts from it, so she sways her hand, attempting to clear it from her face.

"Hi, I'm Hailey." She outstretches her hand to Jensen, then introduces herself to Austin and Gareth next.

My heart thunders in my chest as each of the guys grasp Hailey's delicate palm in their hand, jealousy pulsing that I'm not the one touching her skin.

Needing a distraction, I introduce the guys to Sailor, and Gareth stretches his neck, looking around for his brother and nephew. "Let me go find Bodhi so the kids can play."

As he stalks off, Sailor starts to squirm and asks me to let her down, then takes off running after him, excited to make a new friend.

Her pigtails bounce as she races past the table with the trays of sides we're about to indulge in, and Hailey laughs. "I'll go with her."

As soon as she's out of earshot, the two remaining sets of eyes snap in my direction.

"You didn't tell us about *her*." Austin tips his head at the fiery redhead getting further from view. "No wonder you'd rather be at home than go out with us."

"You invited me out one time," I deadpan.

"Yeah, and you declined."

"Because Hailey had somewhere she needed to be." Why the fuck am I arguing with him? "Help me get the chicken off the grill, would ya?" I thrust the tongs in his direction then glance at Jensen, shaking my head.

He shrugs. "You'll get used to his shit. Apple doesn't fall far from the tree—wait until you meet his family."

"What about you, Jensen?" I ask lightly. "Where's your family tonight?

"Didn't even invite them, Coach. A barbecue isn't worth a trip up from SoCal. Not when we'll be down there next weekend."

"I get that. Are you ready for opening weekend?"

"Yeah, I just wish it wasn't against the fucking Rebels."

"It's too bad they're away games. Can you bring this tray to the table?" I extend a platter piled high with chicken in his direction.

"Yeah, no problem." Jensen takes it from me then stalks off to go put it with the other food, and I can't help but watch him as he leaves.

There's a lot to unpack with him, and I'm not sure what his entire story is—I only know surface level from what he's told me. One thing I know for sure, though, is he's going to be pissed if Owen Marsh does end up getting traded to the Bears midseason like Blake is pushing for. Jensen has never told me why he hates Marsh so much, so as he returns to grab the second tray of meat, I ask him. "What's the deal between you and Marsh?"

Jensen freezes, his face immediately erupting into a scowl. "Why?"

I shrug, nonchalantly, like I'm not thinking about the impending trade. "Just wondering. I know he's an issue for you, and I want to know why." I don't tell him it's because I know I'm going to have to deal with their drama.

Glancing around to see who's near us, Jensen sets the tray back on the small table, then folds his arms over his chest. "I went to college with him and his sister Layla—she was two years our junior. Owen and I never got along, despite being on the same team. He always had a chip on his shoulder thinking he was better than me—loved to talk shit. Dating his sister *really* pissed him off, but when I broke up with her, she turned into a woman scorned, and she and Owen decided to try to ruin my career, and my life."

He shakes his head in disbelief, like he's reliving it again. Clenching his jaw, he exhales through his nose before continuing. "She took false rape allegations to the dean and tried to get me kicked out of school. If I hadn't had a friendly relationship with him, I would have probably been arrested too, but he knows my pops, and he also knows the type of shithead Owen is, so he basically interviewed a jury of our peers, and the allegations didn't stick."

My jaw goes slack. *What kind of asshole goes along with rape allegations just to ruin someone's career?* "You fucking kidding me?"

"I wish I was. It may have happened several years ago, but it's not water under the bridge."

"Can't say I blame you. How old are you, Fields?"

"Twenty-six."

So this probably happened a good four or five years ago. "Well, you're handling it a hell of a lot better than I would in your position. I probably would have gone to jail for kicking his ass."

Now I have to make sure I talk to Blake and try to talk him out of that trade.

Jensen shrugs. "I'm just trying to live my life. The less I have to see that asshole the better, but I give you my word that I won't start shit while on the field. Can't say the same off the field though."

Despite the heaviness in our conversation, Jensen cracks a smile which I mirror.

"Just do me a favor and don't get arrested. We need you out there," I tease, although after hearing his story, I wouldn't blame him if he was tempted. I give him credit for having the maturity to be the bigger man.

"Sounds manageable, Coach." He picks up the tray again, and leaves to go place it on the table.

As he's walking away, Sailor comes bounding back toward me at full speed, and I use my dad reflexes to catch her mid-jump. "I made a friend!" she squeals excitedly.

"That's great, honey." Hailey joins us, and I grin at her. "I take it you found Bodhi?"

"We did and he's seriously the cutest. Him and Sailor get along perfectly. I have a feeling after dinner they'll wear each other out."

"Perfect. Easy night for us."

Us.

Like we're doing this thing together. Like we're coparenting.

Our eyes meet briefly, lingering for a fleeting moment I wish would last much longer.

"Are you ready to eat, baby girl?" I tickle Sailor's tummy, and she giggles as we walk over to the table of food before I pass her to Hailey.

Picking up a steak knife, I clank it a few times against the side of an empty beer bottle sitting on the edge of the red and white gingham cloth. "Good afternoon, everyone." My heart beats wildly in my chest as I address the large group, swallowing the lump in my throat. I hate public speaking, which is crazy considering every game I coach is in front of thousands of people. "I want to welcome you to Coit Stadium, home of the Bridge Point Bears! If you've never seen my ugly mug before, I'm Declan Lane, and as of this year, I'm the head coach."

"More like shit show coordinator!" Gareth calls from a few tables over, and everyone laughs.

My head nods in agreement. "Shit show. Team. Family. However you want to reference the Bears, I'm just proud to be their coach. We have a killer group of ballplayers, and I look forward to a great season. Opening day is next Thursday, and while I'm bummed we won't be playing our first games at home, I'm grateful all of you fine people could join us for our annual celebration today. So eat up everyone, because there's enough food to feed at least four major league teams. Thanks for coming."

The chatter resumes as I close out my impromptu speech and rejoin Hailey and Sailor. Grabbing onto Sailor's small shoulders, I squeeze them gently.

"I hate speaking to crowds," I tell Hailey honestly before I let go of Sailor's shoulders, and grab her hand instead.

"You did great," Hailey assures me. "Truly. I would have stumbled over my words and probably would have started crying, too."

"I don't believe that for a second." Gesturing to where everyone has begun lining up, Hailey and I follow suit.

"Oh, I assure you that's exactly what would have happened. There's a lot of people here," Hailey says, keeping the conversation flowing.

"Yeah, there's a great turnout this year. The last couple of years it's been a lot smaller. I'm glad to see so many people came this time. It's probably because we aren't playing opening weekend at home, though. Been a few years since that's happened."

The line continues to move forward.

"Maybe," she muses, a hint of a smile perking the corner of her mouth up. "Or *maybe* you just have a good relationship with your team, and they wanted to share that with their loved ones."

Her words strike a chord, and I grin like a fool. When

she turns to grab a couple of plates for us, my eyes rove her body.

I can't help it.

She's too fucking sexy.

As she hands me a plate, I know I've been caught looking. Hailey doesn't call me out on it though, and instead she smiles and glances at the ground before reaching over to grab us some forks.

But when her hand meets the basket where the plastic utensils are sitting, she accidentally knocks a few to the ground.

"Shoot," she mutters, then a cold blast of fear sweeps through my bloodstream as she bends to pick them up, and a sickening thud penetrates through the open air as her head connects with the metal folding table.

CHAPTER EIGHT

A sharp pain radiates through my head as I straighten, abandoning the forks I accidentally dropped. My brows furrow as I try to regain my bearings, and I touch my fingertips to where it's throbbing at my hairline.

When I pull them away, they're covered in blood.

Sucking in a tight breath, I stare at them in disbelief before dragging my eyes back to Declan, who looks utterly horror-struck.

For a second, it seems like time stands still, then all of a sudden he springs into action. Grabbing a stack of napkins from the table, he uses them to apply pressure to my head and yells, "Where's Doctor Waggoner?"

There's a slight tremble of panic in his tone, and it sends my heart racing into a frenzy.

A shuffle of footsteps to the side have me turning my

head to see who's approaching, but with the movement comes more pain, and I suck in another sharp breath.

Declan's firm hold never leaves as he applies pressure. "Don't move, sweetheart," his deep voice instructs. The nickname sends the butterflies in my stomach into a complete frenzy.

"Is she okay?" a male voice asks from somewhere behind my periphery.

"Someone take Sailor for me," Declan barks at the men I met earlier, and I realize Sailor is crying.

"Oh, no, Sailor, I'm okay!" I tell her, reaching my hand to her. Her little fingers wrap around mine until someone lifts her into their arms.

More footsteps approach, and a new voice asks, "What happened?"

"I'm okay," I croak through gritted teeth. My hand wraps around Declan's wrist and I try to move him, but he holds steady, refusing to move.

"I'm keeping pressure on this cut until the doctor can look at it."

"Okay," is all I manage to say before another set of footsteps join us.

"What happened?" This man's voice is softer, less concerned and more calm and professional. I assume it's the doctor.

"She hit her head on the corner of this table," Declan

explains. "I haven't gotten a good look at it, I just started to apply pressure to stop the bleeding."

"Good call, let's get her to my office and I'll take a closer look."

"Thanks, Liam."

My hand lifts to my head, and I push on the napkins, trying to get my hand under Declan's. "I'll keep pressure on the cut," I promise.

His eyes search mine and I can see the battle behind them. Reluctantly, he lets go.

The moment his hand pulls away I lose balance, swaying on my feet.

"Fuck," he grumbles, then in one swift movement I'm lifted into his arms bridal style.

Surprise fills me, and I squirm against his hold. "Put me down! I'm too heavy."

"I've got you, sweetheart. You just worry about applying pressure with those napkins. Gareth, watch Sailor for me?"

"You've got it, Coach." Gareth nods, then Declan carries me off, following the doctor.

"You don't have to carry me, Declan, I'm fine," I argue as we cross the field.

"There's blood dripping from the napkins and you practically fell over just now. You could have a concussion, Hailey. So yeah, I'm going to carry you to make sure you make it to the doctor's office without passing out, okay?"

There's a finality in his tone, and rather than fight him, I try to relax in his arms.

It's not a bad place to be, in fact, I've been fantasizing about him touching me for weeks. Granted, I'd rather him be touching me in a different capacity, but considering this is the longest I've felt his skin against mine, I'll take it.

Relaxing a bit, I focus on the small details of Declan Lane. The flecks of gold in his irises, and the way there's hints of copper in his hair from the golden rays of sunshine reflecting against the otherwise dark tendrils. How his body is all hard, solid muscle and even through our layers of clothing I can feel the ridges beneath them and just know he's chiseled.

My breathing changes at the mental image I've created, and I feel the heat rise in my cheeks, so I look away and peer out at the barbecue behind us. It appears things have gone back to normal and the initial concern for my well-being has passed—which is completely fine. They don't need to worry about me, it's just a cut.

Then why do I feel a little woozy?

With one hand, Declan rips open a door that leads into the stadium. Crossing over the threshold, I realize we're entering the locker room, but he takes an immediate left and opens another door.

"You can put her on the examination table," Doctor Waggoner tells Declan, then he turns to me. "Hi, I'm Liam

Waggoner, the team doctor for the Bears. Can you tell me your name?"

"Hailey Shea." Declan sets me down as softly as possible.

"Nice to meet you, Hailey. How's your head feeling?" Doctor Waggoner finishes washing his hands in the small sink in his room and then takes his time drying them with paper towels.

"Not the greatest, but not terrible either."

"Let's have a look." He finishes putting on his nitrile gloves and removes the napkins from my head, then without any hesitation, begins maneuvering my hair so he can see where the blood is coming from. "You got yourself good. It's a decent sized gash—I'm going to need to put a couple of stitches into it to make sure it heals properly."

"St-stiches?" Tears spring to my eyes. "Are you sure?"

"Unfortunately, yes. Probably four, but maybe five. Have you ever had stitches before?"

A hot tear rolls down my cheek as terror seizes me. "No."

"It's a fast fix. I'll give you a local anesthetic, then stitch you back together, and you'll be back out enjoying the barbecue within the next thirty minutes or less."

"Okay." I sniffle, praying to God that my nose doesn't rain snot like it tends to do when I cry. I've had enough embarrassing moments in front of my gorgeous boss, like,

I don't know, the blood dripping from my head right now. The last thing I need is snot, too.

"Not a problem. I have a few forms I need you to fill out since I'm not your primary care physician—technically I should be sending you to the ER for this but as long as you consent to care, it's fine."

"If Declan trusts you, so do I." We make eye contact from across the room and he nods once, giving me all the encouragement I need to let Doctor Waggoner help me.

When he's ready to begin the procedure, he carries a tray to my bedside and sets it down on his rolling table.

Unease grips me as I look over the various instruments he plans to use—a syringe with my injection ready to go, a literal needle and thread to sew me back together. Gauze. A bandage.

Suddenly, the air is being sucked from the room.

"Right, Ms. Shea. Are you ready?"

Slick, hot tears stream down my cheeks and I shake my head, which only intensifies the pain in my head.

"I'll start with an examination to evaluate for a concussion, then we'll work our way up to the stitches, sound good?"

"Okay. Th-thanks." I sniffle again, and the doctor hands me a tissue. It's soft against my skin as I dab beneath my eyes, then my nose. I'm able to calm myself down, and when I give him a tight, forced smile, he takes that as his cue to begin.

After Doctor Waggoner thoroughly examines my eyes with a series of tests and checks my reflexes, I know it's time for the stitches.

I start to panic again. My fingernails dig into the thin paper that lines the exam table, and I squeeze my eyes for a moment, hoping it helps.

Within seconds, Declan's by my side, and he takes my hand in his, trying to bring me comfort. "It's okay, Hailey, breathe. In through your nose, out through your mouth."

He takes a deep inhale, demonstrating what he wants me to do, then exhales. Repeating the inhale, he locks eyes with me, and nods, encouraging me to do the same.

I inhale, then exhale at the same moment he does.

"That's my girl," he praises. "Do it again."

His words cause my heart to pulsate, my toes curling as a warmth spreads through my body, pooling low in my stomach. But it also settles on my cheeks, heating them with both embarrassment and desire.

Modeling another inhale, I follow Declan's lead again, using his breathing techniques to calm myself.

"You're doing so good for me, Hailey. Breathe one more time for me."

Holy shit.

My panties immediately dampen with his praise, my skin growing redder under his gaze.

Oh, I'm breathing all right. Just not in the calm, zen way he wants me to. No, I'm practically *panting* for him.

His praise sends a jolt of electricity through me, and I suddenly feel overwhelmed with desire.

Clearly, it's not gone unnoticed either.

Declan chuckles. "Good to know you like pretty words, sweetheart. Now, give me one more deep exhale."

I release a very unsteady breath, expelling the air from my lungs, embarrassed as all hell but also wholly turned on. It's impossible to focus on anything other than Declan, even when Doctor Waggoner gets to work, spreading my hair around the gash.

"You're going to feel a pinch, then you may feel a cold sensation as the anesthesia is injected. After a few moments you'll be numb in that area and I'll put the stitches in," Doctor Waggoner explains.

Declan squeezes my hand tighter.

I hiss as the needle penetrates my skin. My eyes squeeze shut, but I don't let another tear fall. Instead, I blow out, forcing myself to stay calm despite my instinct telling me to freak out.

"You're doing amazing, Hailey. Keep breathing through it. Squeeze my hand if it's too much."

Declan has no idea his words are straight out of a spicy romance novel, or how utterly turned on I am right now for him.

I don't dare tell him.

And for the next ten minutes I get lost in the

symphony of praise he sings to me as his team's doctor stitches me up.

CHAPTER NINE

The message barely changed to *read* before the phone starts vibrating in my hand. "Hello, sister."

"Hailey what the hell? Are you okay?" Hartley screeches through the phone over a flurry of other voices.

A door slams in the background as she moves to a quieter space.

"I'm fine. I needed a few stitches and some prescription Tylenol, that's all. I promise." Inadvertently, I rub my fingertips against the edge of the gauze that covers my wound.

"Oh, that's all, huh? Like you aren't terrified of blood. And needles. And have the world's lowest pain tolerance?"

She's right, and I know she knows I'm lying. But I don't want to worry her, either. There's nothing she can do from clear across the state.

It's not like I'm in the hospital.

Once Doctor Waggoner was finished putting me back together, Declan insisted on bringing me home. I watched from the bench in the dugout as he said quick goodbyes to a few of his players—shining like the man of the hour when they clapped him on the shoulder, their smiles radiating as they chatted with him—then grabbed Sailor from Gareth.

With his daughter on his hip, Declan curled his hand around mine like it was the most natural thing on Earth, and led us out of the stadium. Sparks radiated through our connected skin and even though we walked through the evening air, a rush of heat coursed through me.

When Declan said he was taking me home, I assumed he meant mine.

But now, I'm curled up on his couch under a plush blanket while he makes us a late-night snack.

"You shouldn't be by yourself," my sister scolds. "What if you have a concussion?" A static-like scuffle scratches the speaker. "Hang on, I'm going to see if there's any flights for tonight."

"You don't have to come up here."

"It's only an hour and a half flight, it's not a big deal." Her voice sounds a little further away—she must be looking up departures.

"No, Hart. I'm not alone." A blush settles on my cheeks, and I glance across the room at the light illuminating from the kitchen. I lower my voice. "Declan brought me back to *his* house. I'm staying here tonight."

"You are?" I can practically hear her smile.

I blow out a laugh, and for some reason, relief cascades through me. "Yeah."

"Hailey Nicolette Shea!"

"*I know*. I told him I'd be fine at my place, but he insisted."

"Well, he's right. You could be concussed. He better monitor you throughout the night."

"Is concussed even a word?"

"I think so. Right? You tell me, miss masters program."

I roll my eyes even though she can't see it. "I don't need to be monitored all night. The whole 'sleeping with a concussion can cause a coma' thing is a myth."

"Myth or not, I still think you're better off not being alone. I'm sure his bed is big enough for two."

"Hartley! I'm not sleeping in his bed," I whisper-yell, looking over my shoulder to make sure Declan hasn't come out of the kitchen.

"No, but you want to be," she goads, her melodic laughter pushing through the speaker.

Groaning, I sink further into the couch cushions. "Shut up."

Hartley snorts. "Where is he now?"

"Making us a snack. I hit my head before we ate dinner."

"That sucks. Oh! Any word on opening weekend yet? Owen said their first four games are against the Bears. Does this mean you're coming down?"

"I thought I told you I was?" My brows furrow, and I pick a strand of the blanket that's come loose. I could have sworn I told her already. "We're flying in Thursday morning."

Hartley squeals in delight. "Does this mean you'll stay with me for a couple of days?"

I wish I could. My shoulders slump. "No, technically I'll be on the clock the whole time watching Sailor."

"So where will you stay, then?"

"Declan booked a penthouse at one of the hotels near the stadium—I can't remember which one. There's two bedrooms in it, so I have my own room, with a private bathroom and a jacuzzi tub! I can't freaking wait for that."

"Sounds romantic. Be sure to ask for champagne service, too," Hartley quips.

She's killing me with the teasing, and she knows it. We've talked numerous times about my attraction to Declan and how I desperately want to know if this is one-sided. She told me to be bold and make the first move, but it's easy for someone who's in a relationship to say that.

"Champagne for one maybe. There's nothing romantic about this trip, Hartley." I catch a movement out of my peripheral. Declan is carrying a tray, coming in my direction. "I'm there to work, and to spend any downtime I have with my twinnie."

"You'd better. I miss you." Hartley sighs.

"I know. I miss you too. Hey, I gotta go, but I'll call you tomorrow, okay? Love you."

"Love you. Make sure that boss of yours takes care of you."

My gaze connects with said boss as he sets the tray between us and sits on the opposite side of the couch. He looks like he's trying not to smile, and I wonder if he heard her through the phone.

"Will do," I murmur, then end the call, and toss my phone to my side.

My mouth waters as I take in the arrangement of food Declan put together. Sliced meats and cheeses, cut strawberries and grapes. Crackers, and cubes of sourdough bread.

He clears his throat. "I wasn't sure what you were in the mood for, so I put together a little of everything."

"This looks divine. I didn't know you were a charcuterie guy."

"I'm a grew up on Lunchables guy. That was the charcuterie of my generation. Although, I have to say, the pizza ones were way better than the meat and cheese ones."

I pick up a piece of prosciutto, a slice of cheddar cheese, and a cracker, and layer it together like I used to back in *my* Lunchable days. "You're right, but the pepperoni pizza ones. Not the double cheese."

He grins, and I feel it radiate straight into my soul. "Obviously. I hope I didn't interrupt an important conversation a few minutes ago?"

"Oh, no, you didn't. I was just updating my sister on what happened. She was about ready to fly up here so I wouldn't be alone." I look down at my lap, and bite my lip, suddenly feeling shy in his presence. "But I told her I was staying here for the night."

The weight of Declan's silence sits heavy. Peeking up at him from beneath my lashes, I'm unsurprised to find him still staring at me. He does that a lot—stares at me. Mostly when he thinks I won't notice, but I always do. It's impossible not to when I can't take my eyes off him ninety-nine percent of the time.

He opens his mouth like he's about to say something, then stops himself, and runs his hand over his beard instead. "Are you close with your sister?"

Something in my gut tells me that's not the question he was wanting to ask.

I study him as he picks up a few berries and a cube of white cheddar cheese. "Inseparable."

"Who's older?"

A smile immediately breaks out across my face. "Technically me, by eight minutes."

"You're a twin?" The look of shock on his face is priceless. It's one I've seen many times over the years. Twins are far more common than people think, but for whatever reason whenever you tell people you are one, they act like it's such a rarity. He mirrors my grin. "I can't picture a carbon copy of you out there walking around."

"Well, we're actually fraternal, so we have different physical attributes. Hartley and I are opposites in so many ways, but identical in personality." Grabbing my phone, I pull up one of my favorite photos of Hart and I, and lean over to show him. The photo was taken last summer at the county fair. Hartley's blonde hair framed her face, her blue eyes sparkling as she stood cheek to cheek with me in that first photo. We're both holding cotton candy in different poses, and as I flip through my phone, it switches like a flip book, changing the way we're standing and holding the spun-sugar treat. "You'll actually meet her on Thursday. Her boyfriend plays for the Rebels."

"Really? Who is he?"

Clicking the side button on my phone, I darken the screen and set it down. "Owen Marsh." The shocked look on Declan's face returns. With a frown I ask, "I take it you know him?"

His features return to stony, and he builds himself a cracker sandwich before he shrugs. "Know of him."

Hmm. Sounds a little ominous, but I decide not to press the issue. What he's heard is none of my business—I'm sure it's just baseball stuff.

"Family is so important," Declan muses, leaning his elbow against the back of the couch. "You're lucky you have a sibling. I grew up an only child."

My jaw slackens, surprised he's opening up to me, but I'll take anything I can get from him. "I'd be lost without my sister. What was growing up as an only child like?"

His answer comes without hesitation. "Lonely."

What do I say to that?

"I'm sorry," are the two words that slip out, and I immediately regret them by the way his face twists.

"Don't ever apologize for something you have nothing to do with, sweetheart."

Sweetheart. There's that nickname again.

"I just meant it in a factual way," he continues. "We traveled and moved a lot, and I was constantly having to make new friends. If I'd had a sibling, it would have made things easier. It's the reason I don't want Sailor to be an only child."

The question that's been plaguing my mind flickers to the forefront again like a neon sign. This time, though, I ask it.

"What's the deal with Sailor's mom?" I blurt, then mentally kick myself. That was *not* the way to ask. "I'm sorry. If that's too personal—"

"How can it be too personal when you care for Sailor day in and day out? You should know about her mother." Declan sighs deeply. "Addison left almost two years ago. We'd only been dating for a couple weeks when she got pregnant with Sail. We tried to make things work, but ultimately she decided her dream of becoming an actress was more important than being a mom. So she walked away. Left her engagement ring, her house key, and a note that said 'I'm sorry. One day I hope both of you forgive me', on the kitchen table."

My hand covers my mouth in awe and annoyance, and as much as I shouldn't be focusing on the words *engagement ring*, I can't help but feel a spike of jealousy.

They were engaged—and she walked away from them *both*. So many emotions are running through me right now but at the forefront is anger. "That's horrible. I'm so sorry, Declan. You and Sailor don't deserve that."

"Addison was Sailor's entire world." He stares off into

the dark with a bit of sadness. "Did you know one year olds understand far more than we think? I watched her spirit get crushed when I told her mommy wasn't coming home. After about two weeks, she finally stopped anticipating the door opening every evening, waiting for her to get home from work. I'm not sure I knew heartbreak until I watched her go through that."

Shuffling a little closer to him, I take his hand in mine. "Does she ever visit? Call?"

Declan looks down at our hands. My heart pounds and I think maybe I've crossed a line—maybe he doesn't want this comfort from me—but he doesn't move it. Instead, he shakes his head. "She'll call every few months. She just did a few days ago, actually, but I've stopped answering. She doesn't just get to pop into Sailor's life whenever it's convenient for her. That's not how parenting works."

"You're right. It's not," I say with conviction. "And I'm proud of you for advocating for Sailor."

"I'm her father. I'll always protect her. Even if it's from the woman who gave birth to her."

Picking up more fruit from the platter between us with his free hand, Declan takes a bite, effectively ending the conversation. Giving him a tight smile, I squeeze his hand then let it go, and scoot back into my original spot on the couch.

Trying to lighten things up, I keep my voice chipper

and playful. "So what's the plan for Thursday, then?" I pick up a piece of salami, and roll it up before I bite it in half.

"We're flying private. Blake bought a team jet, so we'll meet at Valley-Ridge Airport on Thursday morning and head out as a team."

"Is everyone staying at the same hotel?"

"Yeah, we always do." His tone changes mid-sentence, growing more gravely. "I rented the penthouse, like I told you, to make sure we're all together for Sailor's comfort, but so you have privacy."

The butterflies in my stomach stir to life.

For the second time tonight, there's not enough air in the room. It grows charged—electrified. The thought of sharing a hotel room with Declan makes my heart start to pound when it shouldn't.

"Sounds good," I tell him, and it comes out as barely a whisper.

His eyes drop to my lips, and on instinct, my tongue jets out to wet them.

Kiss me. I mentally beg.

Be bold, make the first move, Hartley's voice flickers through my mind.

But I'm frozen in place.

A moment passes by.

Then two.

Then three.

And then it's gone completely.

Standing, Declan shoves his hand through his hair. He towers over me, and—unless I'm completely misreading everything—he's fighting these feelings as much as I am. I can see the conflict etched across his features.

I want to scream, *just kiss me*, but the words don't formulate.

"I should turn in—early morning tomorrow," Declan's voice is strained, and he's suddenly avoiding eye contact. "I'll make sure the guest room is ready, then I'll come clean up this mess."

"Okay," is the only word I manage to say before he gives me a tight smile and practically runs from the room, leaving me in his dimly lit living room on the couch.

I wasn't imagining that—there's no way. He wants me, just like I want him. But he's fighting it.

Now the question is, will either of us ever act on it?

Declan

The team's already warming up when I finally walk my ass onto the field. I'm late, but there was a rollover accident on the freeway causing a huge delay in my commute time.

My duffle lands with a thud in the dirt next to the dugout, a small dust cloud rising above it. Popping open the cap to my water bottle, I take a few long pulls of the cool liquid before wiping my mouth on the back of my hand.

Catching sight of one of my players, Max Callahan, approaching, I close the bottle and toss it on top of my duffle.

He wears a timid smile as he comes up in front of me, raking his hand through his short hair. "Hey, uh, Coach. Can I talk to you for a second?"

Great. Something must have happened before I got here.

Max is one of the most serious players on the team

with his no bullshit, high-drive work ethic. He's closer to my age, in his early thirties, and tends to be my eyes and ears when I can't be. He's played on the Bears for a couple of seasons now, but Blake was considering trading him, and I sincerely hope that doesn't happen anytime soon.

"Of course, Callahan. What's up?"

"Hey! There's the internet sensation!" Austin shouts, jogging over to us. He's wearing a shit-eating grin when he stops in front of me.

"What?" I ask, confused.

"Yeah...that's what I wanted to talk to you about..." Max trails off, pulling his phone from the pocket of his baseball pants.

"You're a viral hit! I'm surprised you haven't heard about it yet," Austin teases me, coming behind me to squeeze both of my shoulders. I shake out from his hold.

"Someone explain. *Now*," I bark, annoyance growing quick like a poison within me.

Max pushes play as he hands his phone to me, and my voice carries from the device. "Where's Doctor Waggoner?" Then cuts to some rap song I don't recognize as the video changes to me carrying Hailey across the field.

One point eight million likes. Six million views.

What. The. Fuck.

"What is this?" I growl, thrusting the phone back into Max's chest. "Who did this?"

"My cousin recorded it, then obviously posted it on

her social media. She had no idea it would go viral, she just thought it was sweet."

"Sweet," I repeat slowly, nodding my head. "And now it's been seen by millions of people."

"On the bright side," Max says through his teeth hesitantly. "The Bears are trending. We're the hottest team in the MLB right now."

"With the hottest coach," Austin adds. I glare at him.

"So what exactly does this mean?" I ask, not knowing what the fuck to expect. Or do for that matter. Am I supposed to put out a statement or something?

"Absolutely nothing, Coach. Now you just sit back and enjoy being internet famous. I bet this will increase ticket sales, too." Austin pulls out his phone and starts looking at something. Then, he laughs, and turns his phone around. "Check it out."

Through narrowed eyes, I look at the screen. It's a map of Coit Stadium showing available seating for our upcoming home game.

Only, there is none...

I whip my eyes up to his. "The game sold out?"

What?

"The next *four* sold out."

The fuck.

"Holy shit." I exhale a breath, and with a surprised chuckle, I grin. "Blake's going to fucking *love* this."

"Fuck yeah, he is!" Austin holds his hand up for a high five, and for once I don't hesitate.

As much as the idea of being viral on the internet nauseates me, I know this type of exposure is going to do amazing things for the season.

"So... You're not mad?" Max raises his eyebrows in question.

"Nah, I'm not. But next time tell your cousin to ask permission before she records me, yeah? Or anyone for that matter."

"You got it, Coach. Sorry about that."

I give him a nod in response, then cup my hands around my mouth and yell to the team. "Huddle up, everyone."

The entirety of the Bridge Point Bears baseball team jogs over to me, and forms a tight circle.

"In less than twenty-four hours, we'll be on Rebel turf for opening weekend. Last season when we played them, there was some tension between the teams. I'm not gonna beat around the bush, so let me remind you guys of this one more time. This is *my* team now. Whatever bullshit Coach Melbourne let you get away with last season won't fly with me. If you're out on the field, have a camera in your face, or even when you think no one's watching, you remain professional. Got it?"

A collective round of "yes sir" is said as I make eye

contact with every single one of my guys. When they fall on Jensen, he smirks.

Narrowing my eyes, I tell him, "Heed my words, Fields." Then, addressing the entire team, I dismiss them to practice.

Heading to the dugout, I slump down on the bench and pull my phone out of my duffle. I don't have any social media, but I want to watch that damn video again so I pull up the search engine and type in Bridge Point Bears to see what happens.

To my dismay, the video is the first thing that pops up with several links to *several* social media channels.

"*Goddammit,*" I grumble, and click on the first one. It's the same video as Max showed me, but this time I click on the comments section. It has thousands of comments, but before I can start reading them, a pop up appears, prompting me to sign in.

Not willing to create an account, I go back to the original page and click on the next one.

Different social media site, same video, but this time there's a woman floating over the video, talking and reacting to what she's seeing. Obviously a green screen, but unsettling to see regardless.

Another link, another rendition of the video.

Finally, I make it over to a platform that doesn't require a sign-in, and I'm able to see what people are saying

—only I quickly learn I should have avoided the temptation of knowing.

Holy shit, the Bears coach might make me a baseball fan!

Off to buy tickets to a game I don't understand!

I guess I'm a baseball girlie now.

I'm no baseball fan but I'd gladly play with his balls!

Daddy? Sorry. Daddy? Yes please.

Sign. Me. Up.

I'd love for him to oversee me on the bench. Or, under me is fine too.

Is this...

"Ah, you've become a thirst trap." Gareth collapses onto the bench next to me, peering down at my phone.

"A what now?" I scrunch my face in confusion.

"It's when thirsty women on the internet turn you into a sex symbol," he explains, and it does nothing to ease the confusion.

"Thirsty?" I ask with hesitation, like I'm not sure of an answer to a math question.

Austin joins us in the dugout. "C'mon. You know what thirsty means."

I tug my cap off and run my hand through my hair. "The internet and Gen-Z slang aren't something I keep up with."

"It means they want you." Austin laughs. "Like, they're thirsty for your—"

I cut him off with a growl. "Do not finish that sentence."

"What Austin is trying to say," Gareth glares at him, "is these women find you attractive and it's really boosting the team's favor this season."

Pinching the bridge of my nose, I clamp my eyes closed. "Shouldn't you two be practicing."

"On it, Coach Hottie!" Austin hops to his feet.

"Austin," Gareth scolds, groaning with annoyance. "Respect the coach."

"I do respect him. I also envy him a little right now." He winks at me, then jogs back to the field.

"Sorry, Coach." Gareth picks up his mitt from the bench.

"Not your apology to give, Fox. For what it's worth, it's not needed either. I've figured out Austin and his personality."

"I know, but there should be a line of professionalism, too."

I laugh. "Professionalism ended when you guys set up that group chat."

"True." He grins.

My phone starts to vibrate in my hand, and I see Hailey's name flash across the screen. My pulse quickens— she never calls.

"Gotta take this," I slur in a single breath before answering. "Hello?"

"Declan, hey," Hailey's sweet voice filters through the phone, "sorry to bother you at work."

My thoughts stray to dark places. *Is Sailor hurt? Is she?* "It's fine. Is Sailor okay?"

"Oh, yes! Sailor is perfect. That's not why I'm calling."

Immediately I relax, exhaling a deep breath as I run my hand through my hair.

"I...um... Have you been on the internet today?" she asks with hesitation.

She's seen the video, too.

"Yeah. A couple of my guys just brought it to my attention. Hailey, I'm so sorry. A family member of one of the players took it and posted it."

"I'm not upset, I just was a little surprised. But I wasn't sure if you'd seen it yet and I feel compelled to let you know *I* wasn't the one who did it."

"Of course you weren't." I'm baffled she'd even say that. "Why would you think I'd accuse you of posting it?"

"I just wanted to be clear that it wasn't me. I don't want you to think I'd do that—try to chase clout or whatever."

My thoughts flash back to the night after her accident where I told her about Sailor's mom leaving us to try and become a Hollywood star. Then I think about Austin's words—*you're an internet sensation*—and put two and two together.

"Hailey, I promise you that wasn't even a thought in my mind, but thank you for the reassurance."

She sighs, and I can hear the relief in her words. "Okay, good."

A tangible silence settles between us and I look out to the baseball diamond where the guys are working on the drills we open every practice with.

It's wild to think that in less than twenty-four hours I'll be sharing a hotel room with Hailey.

And it's even crazier that rather than be focused on opening weekend, our practice, or hell, baseball at all, I'm thinking about the hours of uninterrupted time we'll spend in each other's company after Sailor goes to sleep. That is, if she doesn't immediately retreat to her room in the suite.

"Well, sorry again to bother you while you're working," her voice lulls me from my thoughts.

"Hearing your voice is never a bother." Goddamn do I mean it. I'm so fucked when it comes to this woman, and with every day that passes I feel that last thread of control threatening to sever. I shouldn't have voiced that thought, but I'm having a helluva time pretending like I don't have an interest in her.

A small gasp pushes through the speaker and that sound alone has me growing hard behind my sweatpants. Spinning on my heel, I turn away from the guys even though I know they can't see me. But on the off chance they do look over here, they don't need to see my dick pitching a tent in my pants.

Needing to end the call before her voice alone makes me harder, my voice is far too raspy when I say, "I'll see you when I get home, sweetheart."

My brain should have never given her that damn term of endearment, and now I can't imagine any other nickname for her.

"Yeah...okay. See you then." She sounds as breathless as I am.

I want her. And I think she wants me too.

But if I'm wrong, and I mess this up, I'm not the only one whose heart will be broken. I can't risk another woman walking away from Sailor.

But fuck if I can't enjoy the feeling of knowing that a woman I only imagined in my dreams could want me like I want her.

Call it selfish, but for a few moments, I plan to relish in that.

Feeling on top of the world, I step onto the infield, arms open wide, and project my voice. "Who's ready to kick some Rebel ass for opening weekend?" A round of hoots and hollers echo through the air and it fills me with pride. *Excitement.* "Then let's get to work so we can get home and rest before we fly out tomorrow."

CHAPTER ELEVEN

My palms sweat as I look up the boarding stairs, heart thundering. It's not that I'm afraid of flying, it's just that I don't do it often, and I've certainly never boarded an aircraft from the tarmac.

This isn't your everyday commercial flight.

The Bears chartered two jets to get the team down to Southern California, and because Declan wants his daughter there, I'm about to board with about half the team, and all the coaches.

Declan walks up behind me with Sailor holding his hand, looking like a movie star in his dark wash denim jeans, short sleeve black polo shirt, Bears baseball cap, and aviator sunglasses.

"You okay?" he asks, his free hand ghosting the small of my back.

"Just a little awestruck. I've never ridden in a private

jet," I admit while hiking my backpack further up my shoulders.

"The ones the team charter are usually nothin' special. Especially for this short of a distance. Come on now, let's go find our seats."

The hand on my back nudges softly and I climb the stairs, holding onto the railing as I ascend. At the top, a flight attendant around my age gives me a warm smile.

"Good morning," I greet her as I pass, then my jaw slackens at the sight of the inside of the plane. Nothing special? It's beautiful. New, plush seats in pairs of two that face each other and have small tables between them. Some have magazines, while others have unopened decks of cards. The windows are sparkling, and the flooring looks like it hasn't been walked on.

"Is this plane new?" I ask Declan as I pick a window seat and set my backpack down beside it.

"Not to my knowledge." He helps Sailor up into the seat next to me and fastens her lap belt before he takes off his own backpack and rifles through it, procuring her tablet a few seconds later.

Leaning over, I input the passcode for her while Declan sets up her headphones.

The moment Declan sits in the seat across from me, three of the Bears players walk onto the plane and straight to us. I recognize them from the barbecue—Gareth Fox, Austin Cooper, and Jensen Fields Jr.

"Ay! Coach's here." Austin beams at Declan, dropping down into the seat next to him.

"Hello, Austin," Declan grumbles, but I've been around him enough to know he's suppressing a smile.

Gareth ruffles Sailor's hair before he and Jensen take the seats across from us.

"Well, Coach. Are you ready?" Gareth asks as he gets comfortable.

"I think that's a better question for you guys. How are you all feeling?"

While the men talk about baseball, I find myself studying Jensen. I haven't spent much time with any of these men, but so far, Jensen has been the biggest mystery. Where Austin and Gareth are warm and inviting, Jensen is closed off and quiet. Leaning back against his seat, he stares down at his phone. He's in a plain white T-shirt and jeans, and his Bears hat is backwards. As far as I can tell, he's covered in tattoos. Both arms, with hints of ink peeking from beneath the collar of his shirt.

His energy gives *bad boy*, and I'm curious how he came to be such close friends with Austin and Gareth.

If he can feel me watching him, he doesn't say anything, but as he presses the side button on his phone and lowers it to his lap, I divert my attention to Sailor.

"Good morning!" a feminine voice singsongs, stepping closer to where we're all seated. "My name is Lindsey, and I'll be one of your flight attendants today. We'll be ready for takeoff in about ten minutes, and once we start taxiing, we'll go over the safety procedures. Is there anything I can get for any of you to drink in the meantime?"

"Water, for me please, and an apple juice for my girl," Declan answers immediately.

Lindsey's eyes meet mine, ready for my order. "Diet Coke, please."

She nods, then looks at Gareth. "Water."

"Water," Austin repeats.

When she gets to Jensen, I watch her eyes sweep over him appreciatively.

"Same," he grunts, then glances beyond her as another teammate makes his way onto the plane.

"I'll be back shortly!" Lindsey smiles and goes to the back of the jet.

The guys start talking about baseball again so I reach into my backpack and pull out my headphones. Turning them on, I place them over my ears then pull up the audiobook I was listening to. Typically audiobooks don't hold my attention but I'm halfway through *The Nightmare King* by Kat Blackthorne and I'm absolutely obsessed—I can't stop listening.

Closing my eyes, I let the book pull me into the story until I'm watching Lucy and Mare come to life in my imagination. And before I know it, we're twenty-thousand feet in the air.

"Wow," I gasp under my breath as Declan, Sailor, and I step inside of The Winslow Hotel, a fifty-story building centered in the heart of downtown Rosemoor.

Growing up in Southern California, we visited Rosemoor once or twice a year for beach vacations, but never spent much time downtown because it just wasn't safe. I'm surprised to see such a luxurious hotel here now, but from what I could tell from the short drive from the airport, Rosemoor is trying to change their reputation.

Pristine, oversized white and silver tile floors complement the spectacular vaulted ceilings of the lobby. Everywhere you look is glittering from crystal chandeliers and silver accents shined to perfection. Plush, ruby red couches frame the seating area, facing the reception desks, but the showstopper is the three-tiered fountain in the middle.

Pulling out of Declan's grasp, Sailor sprints to it, her tiny hand dunking in the water before either of us can react. Abandoning the suitcase he's rolling, Declan jogs over and swoops her into his arms.

She hangs in his hold playfully, dipping her head back and giggling as he lightly tickles her stomach. "Daddy, I want to touch the water!"

"Maybe we can go swimming in the pool later. Not in

the dirty fountain." Placing her onto her feet, he grabs her hand again, then reaches for their shared suitcase.

I reach for it at the same time, and my fingers grip the handle first. "Let me get it. You take care of Sailor."

"Absolutely not." His response is immediate, and a jolt of electricity sparks through me when he clasps his fingers over mine. "I already feel guilty I don't have a third arm to manage your bag, too. You're not taking mine."

The conviction in his eyes takes my breath away and I release the handle, but don't move my hand. The little voice inside my head is screaming, *Hold his hand, see what he does!* But I ignore her.

Still, every nerve ending in my body is sizzling with a heat I feel creeping onto my cheeks.

"We should check in," he murmurs, his voice tight like he's holding himself back from something.

My head nods on its own accord. "Yeah. Let's get Sailor settled."

"I want to swim," Sailor whines, tugging on Declan's hand.

"In a while," he promises, then together they walk over to the reception desk.

"Welcome to The Winslow Hotel. Checking in?" We're greeted by a man in a three-piece suit with an eyebrow piercing. Kail, his name tag reads, and I can't help but hold in a laugh because even behind his uniform I know he fits the perfect hipster Southern California persona. I immediately want to be his best friend and introduce him to Hartley.

"Yes. Declan Lane."

"Wonderful." Kail types Declan's name into the computer. "Perfect, here you are. King suite for three nights."

"What? No. I booked the penthouse."

Kail's eyes dart from Declan to his computer screen. "Unfortunately, that's not what I have here. Let me see..." his voice trails off as he concentrates, clicking his mouse furiously.

Declan drops Sailor's hand and pulls his phone out, his attention completely diverted from his daughter, so I pick her up and put her on my hip.

"No, see, right here my confirmation says penthouse." Declan turns his phone, holding it out for poor Kail, who's now visibly nervous, to see.

"Let me call my manager over to help."

Three minutes later, a balding older man power walks over to us, smiling in an overenthusiastic way. "Hello, hello! Welcome, welcome! What seems to be the trouble?"

Kail brings his manager up to speed, and he starts clicking through the computer prompts, as though the answer to the problem might magically appear.

"Hmm," he hums, and I briefly wonder if he has a stylish name, or if it's something like Bob or Larry. "It seems as though we've overbooked the penthouse and the system automatically placed you in our next best room, which is an ocean view suite with a king-bed and a pull-out couch. I understand it's not the penthouse, but I assure you, Mr. and Mrs. Lane, this suite is quite luxurious."

He thinks—oh.

"We're not married," Declan and I say at the same time. I blush when our eyes meet briefly as he continues overexplaining. "She's my daughter's nanny. I booked the penthouse for the convenience of the dual bedrooms."

"I see." The manager sympathetically nods profusely, staring at the screen. "I'm so sorry."

"Let's just book an additional room or suite, then," Declan grumbles, placing his phone down on the counter a little too roughly. The manager startles.

"Sir, I'm so sorry, but we're at capacity." He taps his finger against the top of the mouse nervously. Behind him, Kail is stone-faced but watching closely.

Maybe he's a new hire.

Declan pinches the bridge of his nose. "What do you mean at capacity?"

"We have no additional rooms available."

I can see Declan's frustration bubble to the edge of his patience, threatening to spill over. Placing my hand on his arm seems to ground him slightly, and he looks down at it, before connecting his gaze to mine.

"It's okay. We'll make it work. You and Sailor take the bed, I'll take the pull-out couch."

"You were supposed to have your privacy at night, Hailey. You've been talking to Sailor about that jacuzzi tub for a week now."

"I'll just visit the one at the pool. No big deal." I smile, hoping to drive home my point.

"For the inconvenience, I will apply a two-hundred and fifty dollar credit to your room to use on whatever amenities you'd like—room service, the spa. Just give them the room number and it'll be taken care of," the manager offers with a small smile, clearly nervous Declan won't agree to their olive branch.

Declan looks at me. "I wanted this to be enjoyable for you," he says in earnest.

"I'm already having a great time. Plus, I'm working, remember? As long as I have this girl by my side, I'm enjoying my day." I grab Sailor's ponytail and twirl it around my finger.

Mistakes happen. I completely understand why Declan's upset, but it also isn't anyone's fault.

After a short stare off, Declan must determine I'm not lying to him, and he turns back to the manager. "Five-hundred in credit, because you owe her," he gestures to me, "as much food, champagne, and spa services as she can enjoy while we're here."

"That sounds reasonable, sir."

A few minutes later we're handed our room keys and set off toward the elevator. Sailor bounces on the balls of her feet in excitement as we ascend, and she counts the numbers of each floor as they flash above the door.

We find our room easily and when Declan places the keycard against the lock and the light turns green my nerves detonate.

Gesturing Sailor and me in first, we step inside together and Sailor rips her hand from mine, running over to the floor-to-ceiling window overlooking the ocean. Both of her tiny palms press against the glass, and she giggles with glee.

Leaving my suitcase against the wall, I join her, squatting down to look at her level. "This is so pretty. Do you see the ocean, Sailor?"

"I really want to go there, Mama."

Behind me, Declan drops something, the resounding clatter hitting the carpeted floor.

With wide eyes, I look over at him. I'm at a loss for words—she's never called me Mama before.

There's shock across his features, too.

My brain flips rapidly through everything I've learned in the last several years of child development classes. Would it be beneficial to correct her? Would she feel shame from it? I can't remember, and I'm growing more nervous by the second, wondering what's going through Declan's head, but he's as silent as I am. Finally—although it's probably only been less than a minute—I decide to gently correct her. "Sailor, I'm not—"

Declan cuts me off. "We can go there, Sail. Maybe later."

He doesn't correct her. Doesn't remind her that I'm not her mama, I'm her nanny. He just looks at me so intensely, I feel the heat rise in my cheeks for the umpteenth time.

I'm never not blushing when I'm around this man, and maybe I'm overthinking it, but not correcting this has me wondering if he's considering more between us.

The thought has my pulse racing—another thing that happens frequently around Declan Lane.

"I want to go now," Sailor whines. Stomping her foot, she crosses her arms and worries her bottom lip. Tears line her eyes, and I glance down at my watch—as I suspected, it's past the time when she usually naps.

Scooping her into my arms, I take her over to the bed and gently lay her down in the middle. Taking her shoes off, I tell her, "Your dad has to work later, so when he goes to the stadium, you and I will walk down to the ocean, okay? We can find a treat too, but first, time to rest your body. You don't have to sleep, but we need to have a calm body for a little bit."

"Okay," she agrees.

Declan pulls Snug-Bug out of her backpack and tosses it to me, grinning when I reach out and catch it without hesitation.

Making kissy noises, I make Snug-Bug smooch Sailor's cheeks, nose, and forehead before settling it in her arms.

Pushing her thumb between her lips, she turns onto her side and waits for me to give her light tickles against her back.

While I soothe her to sleep, I can feel Declan watching me, but I focus on Sailor instead of turning to face him.

A million questions wander through my mind, but they're not all questions directed at him. Instead, I'm asking myself some questions, too.

Sailor referring to me as Mama is not entirely unexpected. It's not unusual for a child to refer to a maternal figure in their life, such as a caregiver or a teacher, as Mama. It happens all the time in childcare and preschool, whether the child sees that person in their life as a motherly figure or if they simply get confused.

What has me rattled isn't Sailor calling me Mama, it's Declan's reaction—or lack thereof.

Maybe he was just processing it. Or maybe he was afraid of how I'd react and was waiting to see.

But ultimately the question that burns brightly through my thoughts as Declan unpacks his and Sailor's suitcase, and I lay here rubbing her back and pretending he isn't in the room, has nothing to do with his reaction, and everything to do with mine.

If things were to change between Declan and I, would I be ready to be a mother to this little girl?

Because there would be no in-between. Sailor doesn't deserve another woman walking out of her life, and I would never do that to her.

This is a jump right into the deep end and learn to swim situation, but I can't see the bottom.

What scares me isn't the commitment crossing that threshold with Declan would bring.

It's that deep in my heart and soul, I already know without a shadow of a doubt that I would dive right in.

CHAPTER TWELVE

Declan

It's early evening when I get back to the hotel room after meeting with the team, and my stomach is turning sour from how hungry I am.

It's quiet when I walk into the suite. The lights are off, and as I remove my shoes and kick them over by the bed, I realize the soft noise I'm hearing is the faucet in the bathroom.

Approaching the cracked door, I rap my knuckles against it. "Hello?"

"Daddy!" Sailor's voice squeals, and as I push open the door, I find her covered in bubbles in the bathtub. They're piled on her head, hanging from her chin like a beard, and covering her body from her collarbone down.

Next to her, Hailey is on her knees on the floor with a bar of soap in one hand and washcloth in the other. Water runs down her wrists to her elbows, and she's somehow ended up with remnants of bubbles in her hair.

"You girls look like you're having fun. What'd you do today?"

"We went to the ocean, Daddy!"

"No way!" I feign disbelief and watch Sailor's eyes light up like she's about to tell me the most adventurous story. Of course, I already knew they were at the beach. Hailey sent me several pictures of Sailor running away from the waves, too scared to even put her toes in the water because it was chilly. She's very much a lover of hot water only—doesn't even like to get in pools unless they're already lukewarm.

Can't say I blame her, though.

"Did you play in the sand?" I ask, and Hailey laughs.

"That's why she came straight to the bath! She wouldn't swim in the ocean, but she certainly tried to swim in the sand. It's even in her ears."

"I buried myself! The sand was warm."

Leaning against the bathroom wall, I cross my arms over my chest. "I'm so glad you had a good day, baby girl. Did you guys have dinner yet?"

"I ordered room service," Hailey says, then smirks. "I have to put that credit to good use. Got you a burger with everything on it, and a side salad. Everything should be here soon."

She ordered me dinner? Fuck, she's perfect. "That

credit is supposed to be for your spa treatments, not dinner."

"Declan Lane have you not figured out yet that the way to my heart is through a good meal? Although a massage is an easy way to get in there, too." The way she looks at me tells me she means exactly how it's coming out. She's giving me pointers on how to get her to fall for me, almost like she knows I want to let myself so damn bad.

Her green eyes bore into mine, sparkling as she works hard for her expression to give nothing away.

"Schedule a massage for tomorrow," I urge.

"But the game—"

"Doesn't start until four. I don't need to be at the stadium until two. Schedule one."

"If you say so," she concedes. There's a small upturn of her lips as she adds more soap to the washcloth she's still holding, presumably getting ready to scrub Sailor down.

Ever since I witnessed her reaction to the way I encouraged her while she got her stitches, I've had a theory about the effect my words had on her. So although I know this will have me tip-toeing over the line yet again, I say with approval, "Good girl."

Her gaze snaps back to mine, and a blush settles on her cheeks in a deep rouge, only solidifying my suspicion more.

Hailey has a thing for praise.

God, I want to take her face between both of my hands and kiss her hard.

The only thing holding me back from crossing the room and just doing it is the stark reminder, who is splashing water all over the expensive hotel bathroom.

With a sigh, I look down at Sailor, effectively cutting off my improper thoughts about Hailey. "Hey now, I'll take a shower when you're all done. No need to cover me in bubbles, little girl." I wiggle my finger at her like I'm being stern, but we both know I'm not.

Sailor has me wrapped around her finger and she knows it.

And uses it to her advantage.

"Come on girly pop, let's wash your hair." Hailey abandons the washcloth in her hand and adds shampoo to it instead, while Sailor turns in the tub, shifting so Hailey can wash her hair thoroughly.

It's a routine they've clearly perfected over the months Hailey's been with us. It's hard to believe that she hasn't been a permanent fixture in our lives with the way she handles Sailor. She's a natural.

"You're going to be an amazing mom one day," I blurt before I can stop myself.

I'm not sure why I say it—I don't even know if Hailey wants children of her own, but there's a part of me that wants to know if children are in her future.

She looks a little gobsmacked and bites down on her lower lip, fingers still hard at work massaging Sailor's scalp. "Thank you."

"Do you want kids?" *Fuck, stop talking Declan.*

But it's too late to take it back, and as inappropriate as it feels to be asking my goddamn nanny these questions, I'm telling myself it's not a big deal.

Hailey and I are friends, right? Kind of?

She focuses on rinsing Sailor's hair, gently leaning her back beneath the running water as she cradles her head, running her fingers through the strands with the other hand to remove the soap.

Her lack of response has me growing anxious with the need to know. My mind's spiraling, and in the mere seconds of silence I'm envisioning a life with her—filling her and creating a child with her. Her stomach swollen as he or she grows. Us becoming parents, *together*.

I've always wanted more kids, and I need to know if she wants them, too.

Even if I can't be with her, and I can't because I'm not willing to jeopardize the relationship she has with Sailor, I can let myself pretend and soak in the moments of happiness the thought brings me, if only in my mind.

"Yeah, I do. I love children, it's why I decided to go into the field of early childhood education. I love being around littles." She turns the water off and helps Sailor sit upright in the bath again, hair clean. "What about you?" she asks quietly.

"Yeah, I do too."

She glances at me again before helping Sailor from the bath, wrapping a plush white towel around her. We don't exchange any more words, and I can see her focusing on Sail, so I quietly leave.

There's a lump in my throat as I walk over to the sleeper sofa, deciding to busy myself by setting it up for Hailey to sleep on tonight.

Tossing the cushions near the desk, I realize she'll need linens and walk back over to the small closet next to the bathroom. The girls aren't in my line of sight, and although I'm not trying to eavesdrop as I grab a fitted sheet, pillow, and blanket, I can't help it. I always listen when my daughter speaks.

"Can we go to the beach again tomorrow?" she asks with excitement.

"Probably not, sweet girl. We'll be at the baseball stadium most of the day. Don't you want to watch Daddy's team play?"

"Yes! Can I get a hot dog, too? Daddy says I'm only allowed to eat them when I'm watching baseball."

Hailey laughs. "He's right. You shouldn't eat too many hot dogs. You'll get a tummy ache. Arms up."

The rustle of fabric muffles Sailor's grumble of disapproval.

"Guess who you get to meet tomorrow?" Hailey says with the same level of excitement as Sailor had over the beach.

"Who?"

"My sister!"

"You have a sister?"

"I sure do. She's my twin. Do you know what a twin is?"

Her response is silence, and I rack my brain wondering if she would know what a twin is. I don't remember ever explaining it to her, and I know for certain she's never met anyone that was a twin.

"A twin is when a mommy has two babies in her tummy, and when you're born, a brother or a sister is also born on the same day as you." I can hear a hairbrush being run through Sailor's hair, and I am tempted to peek around the corner, but don't. "Sometimes twins look the exact same, and sometimes they don't. My sister and I don't look the same, but we were born just a few minutes apart." Her explanation is perfect, but why wouldn't it be? She's studied how to speak to children for years.

After a few seconds, Sailor asks, "What's her name?"

"Her name is Hartley. And you know what? She can't wait to meet you."

With a smile on my face, I stop listening to their conversation and go back to the couch, ready to get it set up for Hailey. I put the linens on the desk, then take a quick look at the instructions sewn into the inside of the couch, and reach down to extend it.

Only to discover that the damn thing won't pull out.

CHAPTER THIRTEEN

"Goddammit," Declan curses at the exact moment I steer Sailor out of the bathroom.

He's wrestling the pull-out couch, wiggling the metal frame while he tugs. His grip is so tight that the veins in his forearm bulge while he fights against the resistance it's giving him.

"What's wrong?" I ask as I scoop Sailor into my arms and deposit her on the bed. She gets comfortable sitting crisscross-applesauce, grabs the worn copy of *The Little Mouse, the Red Ripe Strawberry, and the Big Hungry Bear*, and starts flipping through the pages.

Walking over to Declan, he glances up at me and wipes at his brow. "Can't get it to open."

"Can I try?" I'm sure I won't get it either, but maybe it'll be like a jar of peanut butter. Those always open when the second person gives it a go.

He steps aside, letting go of the metal handle, and grunts. Clearly, he's frustrated, so I don't take his sudden flat tone personally.

After a few tugs on my end, it's easy to conclude I'm not having any more luck than he did. Letting go of the handle, I shrug. "It was worth a shot."

This earns me a small laugh, and he gives it another try, putting all of his strength behind it.

When it doesn't budge, he lets out an exasperated breath of air. "Fuck. Of course, the pull-out is broken. Is there *anything* this hotel can do right? I'm going to call the front desk."

I'm not sure what they'll do with no other rooms available, but I keep my mouth shut and join Sailor on the bed, mimicking her posture.

"Yes, this is Declan Lane in room twelve-fifty-six. I'm calling because the sleeper sofa won't pull out."

His back is to me, but it's not difficult to see how tense he is as he listens to the person on the other end of the line.

"Yeah, I've tried that. It's jammed."

Scooting behind Sailor, I start braiding her damp hair.

"We can't just get a replacement brought in?" His hand flies into the air. "Look, we've already had our hotel room messed up because someone overbooked, and now we can't get the pull-out bed to open. We need a minimum of two beds, and you put us in a King Suite with a sleeper sofa."

He looks at it, then his eyes meet mine. Keeping the phone cradled between his head and his shoulder, he fists his hair and shakes his head at me.

Then he hangs up without another word to the person at the front desk.

"There's nothing they can do," he grumbles, pinching the bridge of his nose. "I'm so sorry, Hailey." His eyes shut, and a guilt settles over me, like I'm trying to take it from him. It's not his fault, but he feels like it is. And that makes me feel awful, too.

Neither of us will fit on the couch—only Sailor will.

There's a slight tremble in my hand as I tie off her braid with an elastic and lift my chin, trying to exude far more confidence than I feel.

"It's fine," I tell Declan. "We can share the bed."

His eyes snap open. "What?"

I shrug. "We can share it. It's not a big deal. Sailor will fit perfectly on the couch, and the bed is a king. Plenty of room for us to each take a side."

My heart thunders with every word, but I somehow make it through that suggestion with a steady tone.

Declan doesn't have a chance to respond. He only narrows his eyes as though he can't quite believe what I said and is trying to fully process it, before there's a knock at the door.

In three strides, he yanks it open and is greeted by room service. I jump to my feet and rush to my wallet to tip them, but Declan beats me to it, shoving a bill into the guy's hand before sending him on his way.

He practically slams the door, irritation still rolling off him in waves, and pushes the room service cart further into the room.

"Tip was supposed to be on me." I smile softly, trying to lighten his mood.

"As if I'd let you pay for anything, Hailey."

"Hey, now. I'm a strong, independent woman," I tease, and watch him set Sailor's dinner up at the desk.

"Didn't say you weren't, sweetheart. I just said you aren't paying for anything."

"So chivalrous," I quip, pulling the top off the other two serving plates. Our burgers look amazing, and my stomach rumbles in appreciation.

Declan grunts, then walks over to me and swipes a French fry, popping it into his mouth. Before he reaches for his food again, though, he goes and arranges the cushions back on the couch so we have somewhere to sit.

When I finally bite into my burger a few minutes later, I stifle a moan. It's divine. I didn't realize room service could be so delicious, or maybe I'm just that hungry. Moaning into my burger again, I realize Declan's eyes are on me. They dip to my lips before meeting my gaze, and he swallows hard. "I don't want you to be uncomfortable, Hailey."

My head cocks in confusion. "Why would I be uncomfortable?"

"Sleeping in the same bed as me."

"Oh," I say quietly, lowering my burger back to the plate. "Declan, we're both adults. It's not that big of a deal."

Wrong. It's actually a huge deal, but I'm not going to tell him that. I'm going to be mature about this, and in a little while, I'll crawl under the covers on my own side of the bed. I'll read my book, then fall asleep like I do every other night.

The only difference is that there will be a man on the other side of the mattress.

A gorgeous, older man I'm feeling way too many things for, but he doesn't need to know that.

Wanting to prove to him how unbothered I am by the situation—because hot and bothered is not the same as unbothered—I purse my lips, pretending to think critically, then with all the seriousness I can muster, I say, "We can build a pillow wall."

He nearly chokes on a bite of his burger with a hearty laugh. "Afraid you'll end up on my side, sweetheart?"

Yes.

"No." But my blush deceives me. I feel the heat rise up my neck, giving me away.

Declan smirks and keeps eating.

And I can't stop staring at him as he does.

My thoughts shift to a very, very, inappropriate place. I've never thought of eating to be erotic, but the way Declan's lips curve around the bun, and the way his tongue jets out between his lips after each bite, have me squeezing my legs together.

Suddenly, I'm not so sure if sharing a bed with him is the best idea after all. I have no doubt he'll be a perfect gentleman all night—his hesitation to sleep together is written all over his face—but *I*, on the other hand, should probably take a break from reading the smut I'm in the middle of and switch to a thriller.

Otherwise, I'm not sure I'll make it through the night keeping my hands off my boss.

Because we're all in the same room, Declan lets Sailor stay up past her bedtime and watch a movie on her tablet. She's cozy on the couch, cradling Snug-Bug while she fights against her body's instinct of sleeping, determined to continue watching another Barbie movie.

I've just finished taking off my makeup, ready to hop in the shower and crawl into the giant bed to get lost in the high-thread-count linens. Kneeling on the floor, I flip open my suitcase and rifle through it, finding a fresh pair of panties and my sleep shorts, then dig around for my shirt. Since we're only staying two nights, I didn't feel the need to pack multiple sets, and now that I've reached the bottom of my bag, I wish I had.

"Shit," I mutter under my breath as I push a sundress with embroidered daisies to the side.

"What's wrong?" Declan asks, not missing a beat. He's already kicked back on his side of the bed, wearing a white T-shirt and a pair of gray sweatpants that leave little to the imagination.

I'm no better than a man, I swear.

"I guess I forgot my pajama shirt at home." I toss a few more things to the side and sit back on my heels.

"Need to borrow something?" He's already kicking his legs over the bed when he asks, and crosses the room to his suitcase.

"It's fine, I can make do." But I really can't. My options are limited to a dress, what I wore today, and a couple of nice blouses that are adorable during the day, but would be horrific to sleep in.

I opt for a soft yellow shirt with ruffled sleeves and a V-neck, then stand back up.

"Don't be silly. I packed an extra button-down in case the team did a nice dinner one of the nights, but I doubt that'll happen." He outstretches his hand with the shirt in his grasp, urging me to take it. "You can sleep in it."

"Are you sure?" I'm hesitant, but I reach for the shirt.

Our fingers brush as I take it from him, and for a second, it feels like we get lost in each other's orbit.

"Thank you," I say a little too breathlessly, and quickly stand. Heat rushes through my body, and internally, I groan, knowing tonight is going to be torture. "I'm going to shower."

Declan nods. "Sounds good." Then he returns to the bed and picks up his phone from the nightstand.

The shower does little to ease my nerves, but the hot water feels nice against my skin and helps relieve some of the tension from my shoulders. The water washes away the after-beach smell that I hate so much. You know, the smell of salt water and burnt skin? Yeah, I'm not a beach person, but seeing the joy on Sailor's face made the excursion worth it.

I take my time drying off and dressing, then stare at myself in the mirror. Declan's dress shirt hugs my curves, the fabric taut on my breasts. It hides as much of me as his sweatpants hide of him, but I remind myself that in just a few seconds, I'll be in bed, hidden under a plush goose down comforter.

Relief hits me when I walk out of the bathroom and the lights are off, except for the soft glow of Declan's bedside lamp.

"Sailor fell asleep," Declan explains as I cross the room, dropping my dirty clothes into the bag beside my suitcase.

"Oh, good, she was exhausted." Lifting the covers, I slide inside them, then lean over and plug in my phone.

I'm firing up my e-reader and settling in when Declan says, "Thanks for taking her to the beach today."

"Of course. That's what I'm here for."

"I know," he says with longing. "I just feel guilty that I can't be the one to take her to do fun things all the time."

"It's baseball season. Don't be so hard on yourself." I want to turn over and face him, but that feels intimate. So instead I stay lying on my back, and sneak a glance.

He's doing the same. "Dad guilt."

"You can be guilt-free, I promise. You're a great dad. Sailor is so lucky to have you."

Silence stretches between us for a few minutes, then the bed shifts as Declan turns onto his side and turns off the light. "Goodnight, Hailey."

"Goodnight." My heart is pounding as I roll over, facing away from him with my book in hand.

There's no pillow wall between us. Nothing standing between my body and his except an empty space in a king-sized bed.

I'm hyper aware of every breath he takes, and in desperate need of a distraction.

I press the home button on my e-reader and my book, *Only One Night*, reappears in front of me, and I am instantly sucked into the story.

My doorbell rang, but no one was there.

Was it him?

The logical explanation is that it was trick-or-treaters. It's Halloween, and it's late. Teenagers play pranks.

I'm pretty sure I doorbell ditched a time or two as a high schooler.

That made the most sense.

Yet, there is still a small part of me that wants it to be him. I want him to come to me.

I visualize myself opening the door and he collides his lips to mine as he pushes me backward so he can come inside, slamming the door behind him.

I picture his hands wrapping along the hem of my shirt and dragging it up, breaking our kiss just long enough so he can pull it over my head. He tosses it to the floor before returning his fingers to my shorts and pushes them, along with my panties, down my legs.

Then I'd be bare in front of him. Naked, with my nipples peaked and my pussy dripping.

He'll tug me to the kitchen and prop me on the counter before spreading my legs wide, pulling my ass to the very edge. Tilting me backward, he'll lay me down, the granite cool against my back.

And as he dips his head down, he'll stare at me while the first swipe of his tongue sweeps through the mess his stare is creating between my legs.

The bed jostles again as Declan flips. I snuggle deeper onto the pillow and keep reading.

Licking me relentlessly, he'll swirl his tongue around my clit and drive his finger into me, enjoying the noises the wetness of my juices creates. Over and over, adding a second finger, then a third, until I come so hard I scream out into the darkness of my home.

Then I picture him carrying me to my bed, the same bed in which I lie now, my eyes heavy, and my pussy throbbing for a relief only he can grant.

Startled out of sleep, my eyes fly open when a cold hand clamps over my mouth and a firmness presses against my hips. A man is straddling me, his face cloaked in shadow from the darkness and the hood of his sweatshirt. His fingernails dig into my cheek with care—not hard enough to hurt, but enough to give a warning.

Instinct tells me to scream and as I thrash against his hand, I do, but it's muffled, and I know it makes no difference since I live alone.

I stop moving, letting my eyes adjust, and search for the face beyond the hoodie. It's hard to make out his features and I curse the lack of moon tonight. His free hand dusts along the side of my shirt and over to the waistband of my pajama pants.

His touch is tender, featherlight.

He runs his fingers along the sliver of skin that shows between the two garments. "I've been hard all day thinking about you."

His voice is gravely, and my eyes widen as he shifts his hips, letting me feel the evidence of his confession. Adjusting his position above me, he leans closer to my ear. His breath is hot against my cheek and with just the small change in proximity, I feel myself grow wet between my legs, my body reacting to his presence.

"You're so fucking sexy I nearly came in my pants at the sight of you earlier. All day, I've been thinking about how you'd taste. The sounds you'd make if you let me draw them out of you. I couldn't resist..."

When Declan tosses and turns again, I wonder if me reading is bothering him because of the backlight.

"Am I keeping you up?" I ask quietly, pressing my book against my chest.

"No? Why would you be?" His timbre rumbles softly in a whisper.

"I don't know, the light from my e-reader?"

"Didn't notice it at all. I just don't sleep well in hotels. I'll try not to flop like a fish out of water all night."

"That's okay, once I fall asleep, I'll be out. I just didn't want to be bothering you."

"You're never a bother." Gently, I feel the bed dip as he rolls onto his side again, and this time I know he's facing me. "What are you reading?"

I practically drop my book.

What do I say? I can't tell him it's Halloween smut!

"Um, a Halloween book." Perfect. That's enough of a description.

He laughs quietly. "You know it's spring, right?"

"Spooky season is my favorite." And so is reading about a woman getting railed by a man in a mask who breaks into her house.

"Read me some of it."

"What?" I squeak. "Oh, no. I can't."

"Why not?"

Shit. Shit. Shit.

"You wouldn't be interested in it..." I trail my sentence off, immediately feeling like I've backed myself into a corner.

"I like Halloween, try me."

"It's smut!" I blurt, instantly mortified. I've never been so grateful for the darkness.

"Smut? Isn't that like—"

"Yes," I blurt again, evidently losing my filter completely. "It's word porn and I love it." *Well, lay it all out there, Hailey. Might as well tell him your favorite one-handed reads while you're at it.*

Declan chuckles, and when I look over, I see him adjust so he's propped on his arm, staring at me in the dark. "Maybe I'll like it too. Read me some of your book, sweetheart."

CHAPTER FOURTEEN
Declan

Even without the lights on, I can see the apprehension in her eyes, but as she glances from her book to me, then back to her book. Then, in a quick shift, it changes into something else: challenge.

Her eyes dart across the room to where Sailor's asleep on the small couch.

"It's not appropriate," she argues, but there's not a lot of fight in her voice.

"She's out. I can hear her snoring from here. C'mon, let's hear some of this book."

With another quick glance at where Sailor sleeps, she exhales and gives a curt, decisive nod. There's a slight shake to her voice as she starts to read. "It's *him*. There's no doubt in my mind he's who was watching me from the roof earlier today. Or was it yesterday? It's not like I can reach for my phone and check the time. Swallowing thickly, I wait for his next move. My heart hammers within my rib cage as terror clenches me tightly. 'I'm going to take my hand away from your mouth, but if you scream, I'll gag you. Do you understand?"

Holy shit, what the hell is Hailey reading?

"With him closer, I can make out the intense lightness of his eyes, so crystal blue that his irises look fake," she continues. "My heart seizes up, not knowing his intentions, yet I feel myself nod beneath his grasp. As promised, his hand slowly slides away from my mouth and comes to rest around my throat, and he holds it with the same amount of pressure as he did my mouth."

Fuck, now I'm thinking about my hand around Hailey's neck. Would she like that? If I put a little pressure on the column of her delicate skin as my full weight relaxed on top of her delicious, voluptuous body?

"'Who are you?' I croak, my voice coming out strained and distorted. I clear my throat, not even sure why I'm asking when I already know it's him, but I need to hear it. 'Ah, Little Devil. You don't remember me? You put on quite a show earlier...did you think I wouldn't come back?' I'm frozen on my bed. He's sitting back on his heels now, still straddling my hips but not putting his full weight down. From between his legs, he leans forward slightly to continue holding me in place by my neck while his other hand still ghosts my midriff." Hailey's voice strains as she reads, and my dick hardens with every seductive word that leaves her lips.

Who knew reading could be so erotic?

I want to fucking touch her—feel her body beneath my fingertips as she reads this out loud. Is she wet reading this to me? For me? It takes every ounce of restraint not to close the distance between us and plunge my hand into her panties to find out.

"With my eyes fully adjusted, I can see him better. His hoodie is a dark gray, or maybe a worn black. Unzipped halfway, his bare chest is exposed. He's muscular, so damn muscular, and I want to reach up and trace the outline of his pecs with my fingertip."

I imagine her nipples are stiffened to tight peaks, and what it would feel like to trace the edge of them against the fabric of *my* shirt she's wearing. My dick feels like it might combust, and without thinking, my hips rock, chasing a touch that isn't there.

"'How did you get in here?' The words tumble from my lips in a timid stutter. He laughs and presses his body forward against mine, leaning back down to my ear. 'Do you want me to leave?' he whispers. Shivering, I swallow past the lump in my throat. Despite the terror I feel, I give the slightest shake of my head." She stops reading, letting out a small whimper, and the bed moves slightly as she shifts her body. There's no doubt in my mind that her pussy is aching right now, and I desperately wish I could do something about it. But with my daughter in the same room as us, there is absolutely no way I'm so much as touching this woman's face in a platonic manner, and trust me when I say nothing about what I want to do with Hailey is platonic.

Her voice is strained and breathy as she continues, and barely audible. Still, I listen intently, because fuck if this isn't the hottest sexual thing I've ever done and I haven't even laid a hand on her. "'Because earlier,' he continues, 'it sure seemed like you wanted me to come down off that roof and eat your pussy. Or were you hoping I'd fuck you instead?' Pushing his hand into my pants, he brushes his fingers over the fabric of my panties. My hips buck against his touch and he smiles.'"

"Fuck," I growl, losing all control when she reads those last couple sentences.

"Yeah." She sighs, the bed shifting slightly again as she moves her legs. I imagine her pressing her thighs together under the blanket. "I told you."

As discreetly as possible, I reach under the duvet and palm my aching dick. "Go into the bathroom," I demand. I need to see her. I won't fucking touch her, but I need to know this is affecting her as much as it is me.

"Excuse me?" Hailey drops her e-reader against her

chest, but I'm wrestling with the blankets to get out of the bed.

"Now, Hailey."

This.

Fucking.

Sheet.

Finally shoving it off me, I slam my bare feet against the carpeted floor.

"Why?" she asks, but she's already moving the blankets off her and sitting up.

"Because you're right, the book isn't appropriate. And you're going to read more to me."

Stalking to the bathroom, I hear the light patter of her footsteps following behind me. My palm slaps against the light switch, turning it on and casting the room in a warm glow.

Once she's inside, I close the door and lock it for good measure. Sailor's asleep, I'm sure of it, but you can never be too careful.

I walk to the wall across from where Hailey stands just inside the doorway, wanting as much space between us as possible. I *can't* touch her. But that doesn't mean I can't blur the line a little, either. "This is what you read in your spare time, sweetheart?"

She bites down on her lower lip, and with a quick glance at the e-reader in her hand, she nods.

"Say it aloud. Tell me the type of books you like."

"I read romance. And smut. Readers refer to it as spicy romance."

"That's it, sweetheart." I cross my arms over my chest and watch as that gorgeous shade of crimson flames her cheeks again. "How do these books make you feel?"

"Wha-what?" she stammers.

"Do they turn you on, Hailey? Do you get wet reading books like what you're reading now?" I tip my chin in the direction of the device in her hand.

This is it. Best case scenario, she dances across the line with me. Worst case, she quits and files a sexual harassment lawsuit against me.

That would suck.

For a fraction of a second, her eyes widen, and I think she's going to tell me to fuck off, but then she surprises me when she says, "Yes."

One simple word, but it packs a punch.

Yes, she gets turned on by her books.

Yes, they make that sweet pussy of hers wet.

Yes, she's crossing the line with me.

I go all in—at least verbally.

My erection strains against my sweats, thick, engorged, and begging for reprieve, so I palm it openly, adjusting myself before I lean against the bathroom wall. "Be a good girl and take off your shorts."

From across the room, I see her breath hitch. This

woman loves to be praised, and I can't wait to shower her with it.

Hooking her thumbs into the elastic of her barely-there pink sleep shorts, she pushes them down her legs and lets them pool at her feet. My button-down shirt reaches her upper thighs, leaving too much to my imagination, but I don't ask her to take it off.

"Sit on the counter," I command, my voice low and rough. My dick twitches against the thin fabric of my sweatpants, the head practically peeking from the top of my waistband. "Can you see what you reading that sexy book aloud does to me?"

"Yes." She obeys me easily and hops onto the edge of the counter, e-reader still dangling from her fingers. "Declan, this feels...intimate."

"No more intimate than you being in my hotel room —*in my bed*—in those goddamn little shorts. I won't touch you, sweetheart, but I need you to keep reading to me."

Her chest rises and falls in steady motions, a deep shade of rouge splashing across her cheeks. She's silent for a few seconds, holding my gaze, before her head bobs in agreement. "Okay. I can do that." Picking up the book, her gaze flicks across the screen, then she continues where she left off.

"Softly, he dusts his lips against my neck, groaning into

it. 'Did you dirty your panties with your cum, thinking of me earlier?' His finger grazes lower, and he pushes it into me slightly, still covered with my underwear. My back arches as I moan. I still haven't answered him. I haven't said a word. Pushing my hips forward again, I chase his touch when I should be trying to fight him off, trying to get away from him. His fingers flex against my neck. 'No,' I tell him. 'The fantasy wasn't enough.' A wide grin spreads across his face, and I marvel at how ruggedly handsome he is. His eyes so bright and vibrant they glow, his five o'clock shadow adding to his features and somehow enhancing his straight jawline more. 'Of course it wasn't. But it's okay, baby girl. I'm here now. And I can feel how much this pussy wants me.' He pushes aside the fabric with his middle finger and dips it inside of me. 'So perfectly wet, and tight as fuck.'"

I groan, and her words cut off as our gazes collide. Her chest rises and falls in heavy breaths, much like my own.

"You're doing so good, Hailey. Spread your legs for me. Let me see how wet you are."

Something between a moan and a sigh floats past her lips, and she slowly spreads her legs, exposing her center, although it's covered with the white-cotton fabric of her underwear. There's a small wet spot from her arousal soaking through, and I can't help but lick my lips at the sight of it.

I palm my dick through my sweatpants. "Keep reading. Don't close your legs."

"Declan," she whispers like a fucking prayer, her lust-filled eyes grazing my groin before she snaps them back to mine.

Tension blazes through the air and I want nothing more than to close the distance between us and plunge some part of me, whether it be my fingers, my tongue, or my dick, inside of that pretty wet cunt of hers.

"Read," I rasp. "Picture us as the main characters."

Fuck, what am I doing?

"I barely exhale and he's sitting up again, moving the hand that's wrapped around my neck and ripping open my sleep shirt, letting it fall to the side so my breasts are bare. My nipples are already puckered but when the cool air hits them, they harden almost painfully. 'Fuck,' he groans and kneads my breast roughly. He grabs it so hard it feels like he's trying to rip it from my body, but he soothes the discomfort by leaning forward and taking my nipple into his mouth. I suck a breath sharply before it turns into a moan. The pad of his tongue laps at my breast, and he grabs it roughly with his hand again." Hailey lets out another whimper, holding the book to her chest. "Declan, I can't, I'm so—"

"I know, sweetheart. You're making it so hard to hold back. I want to touch you so bad."

"So touch me. *Please*, Declan. Touch me," she begs, and it's like music to my ears. It flairs something inside of me—something raw and feral.

But I remind myself I can't.

I fucking *can't*.

It's not just my heart on the line.

"Keep reading," I rumble, squeezing my eyes shut before I do something we both may regret later.

"'What is your name?'" Hailey's soft voice is strained. "I half whimper, half moan. He releases my breast with both his hands and mouth, and begins pushing my sleep pants down. His eyes stare into mine as he tugs everything down my legs, panties included. My subconscious screams at me to tell him to stop—that this is wrong— but I don't. I can't. I'm too invested, too turned on, and I would be lying to myself if I said I didn't want this. But the fact he hasn't even asked if I wanted this sends alarm bells off in my head. Still, I do nothing, and as he tosses my clothes to the side, I let my legs fall open. He sits back on his heels again and stares at my pussy with a look of raw desperation in his eyes before turning his gaze to mine. 'We don't need to exchange names, baby girl. For only one night, you're mine, and I'm yours. I'll leave before morning and you'll never see me again, but for tonight, I'm going to fulfill your every fantasy. Would you like that?'"

"Why'd you stop?" I immediately ask, wanting more.

"That was the end of the chapter."

Quiet settles between us, every breath we take only intensifies the desire that crackles around us like wildfire.

How the hell am I supposed to sleep in the same bed as her tonight and not touch her? Not sink myself inside of her?

I need to put some space between us. It might make me look like a piece of shit, but the only thing I can think to do is go take a walk. "Turns out I do like your book, sweetheart. You should keep reading. I'm going to go get some air."

"You're leaving?"

"I'll be back shortly. I think it's best if we both cool off for a few before we cross any more lines."

Pushing off the wall, I stride over to the door. With every step, I feel more like a coward, but I have to think about this long-term and not be selfish.

I went too far, and I'd be lying if I said I didn't enjoy every second of it, but as my hand wraps around the door handle, I feel relief pour into me that I didn't physically breach the boundary with Hailey.

She could still wake up tomorrow and quit, but something tells me she won't.

"Declan, I—" She hops off the counter, her bare feet hitting the tile with a soft thud.

"I know, sweetheart." With a tight-lipped smile, I leave the bathroom.

I don't actually know what she was about to say, but I can imagine many ends to that sentence, and in every scenario, I feel the same as her.

Tossing a T-shirt on, I find the darkest corner and

quickly shed my sweatpants, stepping into a pair of jeans instead, before shoving my feet into a worn-down pair of slides. I grab my cell phone off the bedside table and drop it into my back pocket, along with my wallet and room key, and leave in search of the hotel bar.

As I wait for the elevator, I text in the group chat. I'd put money on the guys still being awake and out, being that it's only ten-thirty.

> Anyone up for a drink?

JENSEN FIELDS JR.

> Already two drinks in.

AUSTIN COOPER

> At the hotel's bar, Coach. You joining us?

> On my way down.

GARETH FOX

> Up. We're at the rooftop bar.

Even better. Fresh air sounds like exactly what I need right now.

As the elevator ascends, I debate getting their opinions about pursuing Hailey. I shouldn't. It's inappropriate to talk to my team about personal matters, and I sure as shit won't tell them about what just happened between us, but I can't help but wonder if I'm blowing this out of proportion.

Maybe it's just fear talking, misguiding my subconscious into thinking pursuing her is a bad idea when it could actually be something life-changing.

But if it's not fear, and it's actually intuition giving me a glimpse into the shitstorm of my future, I feel like I should heed its warning.

Either way, by the time the elevator doors open, I decide to see what their thoughts are on it, but first, I need a beer or two.

CHAPTER FIFTEEN

"Holy shit, Hailey, VIP box seats?" Hartley trails her finger against the open rail overlooking the baseball diamond. We're practically on the field, right next to the dugout, with the perfect view and a full waitstaff.

"Does Owen not get you box seats when you go to games?" I ask, watching her with wide-eyed wonder. My sister shakes her head, and although there's a smile on her face, I can see the sadness in her eyes. She's not fooling me, that's for sure. "Hartley—"

I'm cut off by the shrill sound of Sailor screaming. My head snaps in her direction, and thick crocodile tears stream down her face as she stares down at the hot dog—covered in ketchup, mind you—sitting upside down on her brand new dress. There's no way it isn't ruined.

"I'll go grab some napkins." Hartley rushes out the

door separating our box from the rest of the seats in search of something to clean up with.

Rushing to Sailor's side, I kneel down, picking up the hot dog with one hand and squeezing her knee with the other. "Oh no. What happened, Sail?"

"It fell." She sniffles, and the sad look in her little doe eyes tugs on my heartstrings.

"That's okay. Accidents happen! We'll get you cleaned up and good as new, okay?"

She nods, and Hartley reappears with a stack of napkins, half of which she's wet with water for me.

"Thank you." I take them and place the dry stack on the chair next to Sailor, while I scrunch up the wet stack and start making circular dabbing motions against her dress.

"Do you want another hot dog, my friend, or are you going to show this one who's boss?" Hartley asks as I do my best to clean Sailor up.

There's about twenty minutes until the game starts, and more friends and family of the Bears start to find their seats, which only adds to the pressure. Why is it so awkward to have an audience when you're trying frantically to clean or fix something?

"Show it who's boss!" Sailor's tears dry up as she starts giggling at Hartley.

"Excellent choice." Hartley uses the napkin she kept in

her hand to wipe off the rest of the ketchup from Sailor's hands, then hands the hot dog back to her.

When things are settled, I retake my seat between Sailor, who's now snacking on popcorn, and Hartley.

"I miss you," I tell her, bumping my shoulder into hers.

"Well, good, because I'm highly considering moving to Bridge Point." Hartley beams, and my jaw practically hits the floor.

"Wait, really?"

"Really!" she squeals in delight. "Isn't your condo a two-bedroom? Need a roomie?"

"You never have to ask! What about Owen, though?" My attention is grabbed by the Jumbotron as it announces the players for the Rebels, and ironically, Hartley's boyfriend, Owen Marsh, comes onto the screen.

She pauses, too, and we both watch as he gives his interview, answering a few goofy questions and flashing a charming smile. When his voice stops booming across the stadium, she turns back to me. "Well, he's pretty certain he's getting transferred to the Bears mid-season. There's been a lot of talk lately, and that's the word on the street. But even if he doesn't, I almost feel like our relationship has an expiration date. One week, he's attentive and loving, and the next, it's like he's erased my name from his vocabulary. It's weird, honestly."

"Do you think he's cheating?" I ask bluntly, hating

that my sister is obviously going through a lot in her relationship. She's told me about it in passing, but for the most part has never been one to divulge a lot of details about their dynamics.

"No? Maybe? I would hope not, but I also wouldn't be shocked, you know?"

"That's horrible, Hart."

She shrugs. "Yeah, but at least I'm not delusional and thinking this man is my forever. He's my right now, and yes, I love him, but he's not my future husband."

"And you're okay with that?"

"Girl, don't judge me. You're the one who's sleeping in your boss's bed."

"Hartley!" Yeah, I might have told her a little about last night. Not everything, but I definitely told her the hotel screwed up our room, that we're bunking together, and that when he came back last night I pretended I was asleep because otherwise my horny ass would have tried to jump his bones. "You know I have no choice!"

"Oh, you have a choice, beautiful sister. You could have gotten a Lyft to my place last night, but you chose to share a bed with the hot coach instead."

Snorting a laugh, I roll my eyes at her and shake my head, grateful that Sailor is engrossed in the Jumbotron.

My sister is right, though—she lives ten minutes from the hotel. I could have stayed with her.

But I definitely didn't want to.

"Do you want to stay at my house tonight?" she asks, her voice light and teasing.

Pursing my lips, I toss a quick glance in her direction, but say nothing.

Laughing, she pats my thigh. "Oh, Hailey, Hailey, Hailey. That's okay. I think Coach has it just as bad for you as you do for him."

My eyebrows crease together. "What do you mean?"

She lifts her chin in a quick jest, nodding to where Declan's standing at the edge of the dugout, his eyes already on us.

No, not us.

Me.

The heat in his gaze makes my pulse quicken.

"Doesn't matter," I tell my sister, without disconnecting from Declan's stare. "Nothing can happen between us."

"Does he know that?" she questions. "Because he's practically undressing you with his eyes in front of everyone, Hails."

Is that what that look is?

The pulse in my core aches in confirmation.

Yeah, that's what that look is. And I'm doing the same thing to him.

Seconds later, one of the Bears' players jogs up to him, and he's forced to turn away, adjusting his hat as he turns to speak with him. And just like that, it feels like something's missing without his gaze on me.

But to answer Hartley's question, which I don't give her the courtesy of answering out loud because I'm ready to put a pin in this conversation, Declan *does* know that nothing can happen.

He's the one who made that abundantly clear last night.

The game seems to fly by, and every spectator in the stadium is on the edge of their seats as the Bears and the Rebels enter the bottom of the ninth, the Bears leading the game by one point. Rebel fans have started a chant to cheer on their team, only needing one run to tie up the game, two to win it.

Even Sailor's fully engaged, munching on her cotton candy as she stands on her tiptoes, peering over the edge of the rail at her daddy.

It's no surprise when Austin Cooper walks out onto the pitcher's mound again, grinning from ear to ear. Excitement trickles through me, intuition telling me the Bears have this game in the bag. Austin's one of the best pitchers in the Majors right now.

The first Rebel up to bat anticipates Austin's pitch with enough precision to hit the ball far enough to make it to first, his strides long and forceful as he runs to the plate.

Groaning, my shoulders deflate a little as the majority of the stadium cheers.

The second batter strikes out immediately, and doesn't even try to hide his irritation as he storms off the field and back into the dugout. It's almost comical, but I imagine the tensions are high right now, and the Rebels' coach must be pitching a fit that the game is this close.

The Rosemoor Rebels aren't just rivals of the Bears, but their coach has been making passive-aggressive digs at Declan and his coaching on every interview I've seen. I'm not sure why he has it out for him so much, but I suspect it's because he knows the Bears have some strong players this season.

A smug smirk graces Austin's face and is broadcast over the Jumbotron but he quickly schools his features and watches as Marsh steps up to bat.

In her seat, Hartley sits up a little straighter to watch.

With a perfect pitch from Austin, Owen swings and hits the ball into the outfield.

I'm up on my feet in an instant, watching Jensen Field Jr. with bated breath as he carefully tracks the ball. The player that was on first is now on second, and Owen's cleats just hit the first base plate.

My hands curl around the railing in front of me.

Jensen makes a few calculated side steps, then catches the ball at the same moment Owen slides into second, and the other guy's a few steps off of third.

Two plumes of red dust float into the air from their cleats dragging across the dirt, but it's too late.

Jensen throws the ball to the Bear on first base, and the umpire calls both out.

The Bears and their fans go wild.

Our box erupts with cheers and screams of glee. Sailor jumps up and down, her hands intertwined with Hartley as they share a moment, Hartley hyping Sailor's excitement up tenfold.

I'm grinning like a fool, my stomach pressing against the edge of the railing as I cup my hands around my mouth and cheer in the direction of the away team dugout.

The Bears are celebrating their win, congregated in a tight circle full of shoulder claps and mitt tossing, when suddenly Declan breaks away from his team, eyes trained solely on me, and jogs in my direction.

My heart erratically beats as he gets closer, wearing one of the biggest smiles I've ever seen on his face. Triumph rolls off him, and in a swift motion, he jumps onto the small lip of the wall, elevating himself to my level. There's no hesitation—no doubt or uncertainty within him—as both his hands grab my face and he slams his lips to mine.

Soft and sure, his tongue sweeps across the seam, parting my lips. It takes a millisecond before I melt, feeling like my entire life has led up to this moment. A calm, steady wave crashes through me, and my body takes over, kissing him back with equal fervor as he deepens it.

The stadium melts away, and for several seconds, it's just us.

Two puzzle pieces that fit perfectly together.

Declan and Hailey.

A moan vibrates through my chest as his tongue continues to explore my mouth, his hand moving to cup the back of my head, holding me in place.

But all too soon, he pulls away, leaving me wanting so much more. In the briefest of moments, he leans his forehead against mine, and I wonder if everything's just changed between us.

"So fucking worth torturing myself over, sweetheart," he groans, making my heart flutter.

Grinning, he ruffles Sailor's hair as she looks up at him, then he jumps down and runs back toward the team.

My fingers reach up and brush my now swollen lips, completely speechless as to what just happened.

Sailor doesn't question why her dad just came up and kissed me, nor does she seem to notice. Thank God, because I don't have a single answer for her.

I'm in a daze, and don't even have it in me to give my sister a reaction when she chirps with an overdramatic sigh. "My hopes and dreams of a sleepover with my sissy are ruined now. Maybe Sailor can take your place—I have a feeling her daddy's going to become someone else's Daddy tonight."

CHAPTER SIXTEEN

Declan

"You need us to watch Sailor for you tonight, Coach?" Gareth jests while we're all in the locker room.

The game is over, our first win of the season against our rivals at their stadium, and it feels pretty damn good. After a closing speech in the locker room, I dismissed my guys and told them to go have some fun—they earned it.

"Yeah, she can hang out with her uncles while you go have a little fun of your own with the nanny," Austin jumps into the conversation.

"You're not Sailor's uncles," I grumble, shaking my head at Austin. "And I'm not going to have some fun with Sailor's nanny."

"Does he have amnesia?" Jensen rubs at his neck with a towel before tossing it to the side and pulling his shirt overhead. "Because the whole world just saw him kiss her, and now he's trying to act like he doesn't have feelings for her."

Fuck. It's that obvious.

"Oh, the world saw it alright." Austin laughs, staring down at his phone. "Guess who's viral again."

"AGAIN?" I boom, ripping the phone from his hand. "How does this happen so quickly? Who the hell recorded it this time?"

"Coach, there had to have been twenty thousand people there today. At least." Gareth looks at me like I'm the world's biggest moron. "I'm sure at least a third of them captured it on video."

Not knowing how to use whatever platform Austin has pulled up, I tap on the screen, and a heart appears across it.

"Scroll," he instructs.

"How the fuck did this happen so fast?" Every other god damn video is of mine and Hailey's kiss.

"Does he not know how the internet works?" Jensen deadpans.

"It just—it—" What the fuck. "I kissed her thirty fucking minutes ago!"

Fucking viral *again*? It feels like a violation of privacy —our first kiss captured on video, hundreds of times, at different angles.

But I'm the dumbass who impulsively kissed her publicly.

Very publicly.

Thrusting the phone back at Austin's chest, I walk out of the locker room.

"Coach!" Austin laughs uncontrollably.

"Maybe she won't care!" Gareth calls with encouragement, but I ignore them all and stomp my ass directly into the sea of fans all trying to file out at once.

Pulling my phone from my pocket, I call Hailey.

Her sweet voice filters through the phone after the second ring. "Declan, hey."

"Hey. Where are you guys?" Her side of the phone is as loud as mine is, clueing me in that she's still at the stadium.

"Trying to get out of here," her voice raises slightly. "Do you want to meet somewhere?"

I lower the rim of my hat, shielding my face as a group of passing women seem to recognize me. "Yeah. Take Sail back to the hotel and I'll meet you at the restaurant."

"Do you mind if Hartley comes?"

With my head lowered, I weave through the crowd. It's practically survival of the fittest to get through this mess. "Not at all, sweetheart. See you guys soon."

About thirty minutes later, I make it to the hotel's restaurant. It was a nightmare getting through the foot traffic downtown, and I'm borderline hangry when I arrive. Spotting their table near the window, I'm happy to see Sailor already has a plate of macaroni and cheese in front of her, and Hailey and her sister have been served some sort of blended fruity drink.

"Don't worry, it's a virgin," Hailey blurts as I slide into the seat next to her sister. I try not to laugh. I wouldn't give a shit if she was enjoying a drink right now—not after this long day.

Does she know about the newest viral video of us?

As I walked to the hotel, I searched through YouTube since I know how to use it, and of course, people are going crazy.

I can't believe this happened again.

"Hi, I'm Hartley." The blonde next to me holds out her hand. "I believe you're pretty well acquainted with my sister, who sometimes has no filter."

I laugh, sliding my palm into hers. "Hi, Hartley, I'm Declan. Nice to meet you."

Her handshake is firmer than I expected it would be. Hartley looks similar to her sister, but with major differences. They share the same eyes and smile, but Hartley has more of a button nose while Hailey's is straight, and Hartley's hair is quite a contrast to Hailey's red. Physically, Hartley is petite and a little shorter, but if I remember correctly, she's a ballerina, which would attribute to her smaller frame, I'm sure.

"Cute kiddo you have. I can see why my sister is fond of nannying for you. That, and the VIP box seats don't hurt either."

"Hartley!" Hailey gasps, looking mortified.

"What?" She shrugs. "Those were amazing seats."

"Well, you're welcome to utilize them at any Bears game. Door's always open," I promise. "Did you ladies order?" Picking up the menu, I scan through it, my stomach panging with hunger as I look over my options.

"Not yet," Hailey responds. "We were waiting for you, but Sailor was hungry, so I ordered hers."

Our eyes meet across the table. "Thank you."

Her lips upturn in a smile, and the urge to get up and kiss her burns bright within me. Like every inopportune time, though, that feeling is interrupted.

"Hello, sir." A waiter approaches the table with his order pad in hand. "What can I get you to drink?"

It's on the tip of my tongue to order a beer, but there's only one thing after a long day in the sun that I should be drinking. "I'll stick with water."

"Is the table ready to order dinner?" the waiter asks, glancing at us.

"Ladies?" I question, and both Hailey and Hartley nod their heads in unison.

I wonder if that's a twin thing.

"Ravioli, please. With a Caesar salad," Hartley takes the lead with ordering, then hands her menu to the waiter.

Hailey orders next, and I try to focus on the menu, but it's impossible when her voice sends my heart into a frenzy. "I'll do the grilled chicken breast with scalloped potatoes and a house salad, please."

"Dressing?"

"Vinaigrette."

"Excellent," the waiter approves. "And for you, sir?"

"Sirloin, please, medium rare."

"Mashed potatoes and asparagus are served with it, unless you would prefer to substitute for a side salad?"

"However it comes is fine. Thank you."

The waiter nods and finishes jotting down everything. "Very good. Your meals will be out shortly."

A round of *thank you's* circulates through the table, and he walks away, leaving me with the Shea twins and Sailor.

"So, Hartley. Hailey told me you're dating one of the guys from the Rebels?" I make small talk as I pick at a roll from the breadbasket on the table. What I want is to talk to Hailey alone, but I know that won't happen until tonight.

"Yeah, Owen Marsh." She pops a piece of bread in her mouth and doesn't elaborate. Not that I need the details.

The rest of our early dinner moves quickly when the entrees come out, and before I know it, it's time for us to say our goodbyes.

Glancing at my watch, I see that it's barely seven—no need for both of us to call it a night so early.

"Why don't you and Hartley put that hotel credit to good use and head over to the spa?" I suggest to Hailey as she scoops the rest of Sailor's macaroni into a to-go box.

Hartley squeals. "I love that idea."

"Are you sure?" Hailey asks hesitantly. There are unspoken words behind those green eyes of hers, and I wonder what they're really trying to say.

"Sure am." I nod as I take the leftovers from her hand. "You deserve it. Take the night off—enjoy yourself."

"I hear this hotel has rooftop bowling," Hartley tells her sister with enthusiasm.

"I can confirm that. There's a bar up there, too." I was up there last night with the guys for a few hours, watching as they played. Thank God they're better at baseball than they are at bowling.

"Okay, if you're sure you don't mind," Hailey finally relents when Hartley laces their hands together and pulls her from her chair.

"Have fun." I smile, then stand too, and go help Sailor up.

"Bye, sweet girl, I'll see you in the morning, okay?" Hailey kisses the top of Sailor's head, then is pulled away by Hartley.

"Where's she going, Daddy?" Sailor asks while we weave our way through the restaurant hand in hand.

"To spend some time with her sister. What do you say we get you in the bath, and I'll order some ice cream to the room?"

"Yes!" she shouts as we enter the lobby and a few nearby hotel guests look in our direction.

The excitement in Sailor's step fuels my own, and I

realize it's been far too long since we've had a relaxed, unstructured night together.

Swinging into the hotel's gift shop, I let her pick out nail polish, and the cashier lends a helping hand by also grabbing something called a top coat for it. I also pick up a pair of overpriced pink fuzzy slippers in Sailor's size, and she picks out a bag of Cheez-Its and a red Gatorade.

Hailey may be off getting pampered at the spa, but I see no reason why Sailor can't have a little spa evening of her own.

There's no time like the present to learn how to paint pink glitter on ten small fingers and ten small toes.

CHAPTER SEVENTEEN

I knew I missed my sister, but the magnitude of how deep the ache was didn't dawn on me until I spent the entire day with her.

Obviously, being a twin naturally means you're inseparable for your entire childhood, but Hartley and I have been inseparable throughout our adulthood as well, up until I moved to Bridge Point to finish college. That decision didn't come lightly, and the only reason I had to stay was because it seemed unbearable to leave her.

In the end, she forced me to go.

We've seen each other a few times here and there, but it's almost as though the emptiness gets buried when we're apart, making it manageable to do the day-to-day monotony without realizing there's a piece missing.

Some call it codependence, but we call it a soul tie.

Mine and Hartley's evening started off with massages,

which we booked as a couples massage so we could chat the whole time. Lying on the massage table with tears streaming from my eyes and onto the floor because of so much laughter was exactly what the doctor ordered, and it made me feel whole again.

After our massages, we went to the rooftop and bowled a few games, enjoying a couple of fruity drinks while groups of men kept making eyes at Hartley. She, of course, didn't entertain them, fiercely loyal to Owen, even though I'm one hundred percent certain he's not loyal to her.

While she drank several drinks, I cut myself off after two in hopes of getting back to the hotel room early to speak to Declan. The unknown of what that kiss meant to him has been lingering on my mind since it happened, making it hard to fully focus on anything else.

I wonder if he knows we were caught on camera and have gone viral yet again.

When Hartley checked her social media, it was the first thing we saw on the home screen. My cheeks flamed as I watched the replay, the moment that I'll forever cherish captured in several different angles and uploaded for everyone to see.

With the first viral video, Declan didn't seem to have too big of a reaction, but with a more intimate moment caught on camera, I'm worried this will force his hand into backtracking on whatever this is between us.

It's entirely possible that the kiss was a one-off. A heat of the moment thing that he never intends to happen ever again.

I wouldn't blame him if it was, but God, I hope it isn't.

Kissing Declan was as sweet as getting caught in the rain on a warm summer night. It made my heart swoon and my panties melt, and was the one thing that finally felt right about leaving behind my life and starting new in Bridge Point.

Now, as I sneak into the hotel room after making sure Hartley was safely picked up by her boyfriend, I know Sailor will be asleep, but I'm praying Declan isn't.

It's past ten, and as I push open the door, the room is dark and quiet—not even the TV is on.

He's gone to bed.

With a subtle sigh, I step further inside and close the door quietly behind me. The lock engages automatically, the electronic mechanism whining, but instinctively, I secure the dead bolt, too.

My steps are quiet across the carpet as I head to where my suitcase is so I can grab my pajamas and hit the shower, but once I'm parallel with the bed, I hear my name.

"Hailey." Declan's deep timber rattles through my heart, and I turn to look at him, my eyes only semi-adjusted, but I can make out his silhouette as he lies in bed. With the blankets pooling around his waist, his Adonis-like chest is bare and on full display as he relaxes with one hand under his head.

"Did I wake you?"

"No." He shakes his head. "I was waiting for you."

"Oh." My voice goes quiet. The only thing I can hear is my heartbeat in my ears.

"Do you want to take a shower, then we can talk?" His gruff whisper sends the butterflies in my stomach fluttering in a frenzy.

"We can talk now." I'd rather use the shower as an excuse if I need a moment. I'm not sure what to expect.

"Okay, let's go into the bathroom so we don't wake Sailor."

My heart rate quickens knowing what happened last time we were in the bathroom together. But I agree, this conversation should be had in private, even if Sailor is fast asleep. On the off chance she wakes up, whatever is going to be said does not need to be said in front of little ears.

With a lump in my throat, I follow Declan inside the bathroom and watch as he flips the lock. No sooner are we locked in, does he take a couple steps forward, his hand sweeping beneath my hair to wrap behind my neck. Before I can articulate another thought, his lips are on mine, claiming them more possessively than before.

He tilts me, bending me to his will, and all I can do is succumb to the high of it all.

If I thought he took my breath away earlier on the

baseball field, I was wrong, because at this point I'm certain the only oxygen I'm intaking is his. My head swims, and a bliss-filled tremor racks through me as I forget all about all of the obstacles standing in our way.

Declan kisses me like I'm the most precious thing in the world, taking his time exploring my mouth, keeping me rooted firmly on the ground so my body doesn't float away in euphoric bliss. A moan rattles through my throat, and I can feel myself melting—my heart transforming into something that only beats for him.

It terrifies me, because then that means he has the ability to break it.

Breaking the kiss, Declan rests his forehead against mine, breathing heavily. "I've been waiting to do that again all day."

"So it wasn't a one-time thing?" I ask hesitantly, squeezing my eyes shut.

We stay pressed together, neither of us creating more distance.

"Open your eyes and look at me, sweetheart." His tone is firm—low and commanding. Something dips in my stomach as I open my eyes, meeting his piercing gaze. "Do you want it to only be a one-time thing?"

"No." The word comes out rushed.

Declan laughs, then kisses me with a soft peck again. Not ready for him to pull away, I wrap my arms around his neck and pull him closer, bringing his lips back to mine.

He groans deeply, then lowers himself enough to lift me into his arms.

My legs wrap around his back, and he carries me to the bathroom counter, effortlessly setting me on top of it. He pulls my hips forward so I'm on the edge, then aligns our groins. His hard length settles between us, and without another thought, I rock my hips into it.

"*Fuck*, you have no idea what you do to me, Hailey."

"I want you," I tell him in a frenzy, my fingers furiously drifting across his body.

He thrusts his hips, his shaft hitting the sensitive part of my body over and over as he glides it against me. There are too many layers between us—his sweatpants, my sundress and panties.

His lips move to my neck, nipping and licking up the column of it as his palm kneads my breast. "You're so sexy. The things I want to do to you—" he groans "—God, I want to taste every square inch of your skin."

"Please," I whimper. My hands trail down to his waistband, and I'm about to reach my hand inside when he catches my wrist.

"Good things come to those who wait, sweetheart." His teeth skate across my skin. Holding my wrist, he gently pulls it behind my back, forcing my back to arch and my hips to push into him further.

We moan in unison at the rough contact.

Pushing my dress to my waist, he bunches it up and

slowly—tortuously—he slides himself against me. The flick of his hips sends an ache through my core every time his length hits my sensitive clit.

I'm desperate for more of him—all of him.

"Declan," I whine, my eyes rolling back.

"You're so perfect, Hailey. Such a good girl letting me dry hump the fuck out of you. Do you like the way it feels, sweetheart? I'm so hard for you. Do you feel what you're doing to me?"

"Yes," I moan. "I want more, Declan. I want all of you. I want you inside of me."

"I want that too, sweetheart. I want nothing more than to have this tight little cunt soaking and milking my dick. I'm going to make you feel so good."

Holy shit.

His words send a jolt of arousal through me, and the telltale signs of an orgasm building tingle. Catching my lips again, Declan kisses me, and it's as desperate as I feel. Full of teeth clashing and heavy moans peppering through every stroke of our tongues. His hips never stop moving, thrusting and rocking against me so intensely, all I can do is squeeze my legs around him tighter and free-fall when my orgasm crashes into me.

Crying out his name, I toss my head back, stars overtaking my vision. He releases my wrist and moves his hand to my hair, pulling my head back to him and catching every whimper and moan I give him through my climax.

His hips work in time with my incoherent chants, and seconds later, he grunts long and hard, his head falling to my shoulder.

It takes several minutes for us to catch our breath. My legs stay wrapped around Declan's hips, my hand on his shoulder as he keeps his head on mine.

"You're absolutely perfect. Trust me when I say that the moment we're truly alone, I'm going to worship your body, sweetheart. I'll take my time with you and give you everything you deserve."

I lean back to look at him, and he lifts his head. His eyes sparkle, and with a quick glance down, I notice his sweatpants are saturated near the waistband from his release, and pride blooms in my chest.

I did that. He wants me just as badly as I want him.

But I still have doubts. There will be so much working against us if we give this a chance, the biggest thing being Sailor. If Declan and I don't work out, how could I still be her nanny? Losing them would be devastating...

But not giving us a chance would be even more soul-crushing.

When our eyes meet, I ask, "You're sure about this? What about—"

He cuts me off with a kiss. "Yeah, sweetheart, I'm sure. I've lied to myself for months about not wanting you, and I'm done. We'll figure it out as we go. This is just the beginning for us."

The planes that were chartered for the team to go home were smaller than the ones we arrived on, so Sailor and I flew commercial. Despite Declan's protests of staying with us, I convinced him to go with the team and that we'd be fine. Little did I know we'd be delayed until the turn of the century, but it was fine. Sailor and I enjoyed some nachos in the airport, watched a couple of movies on her tablet, and shopped in just about every store they had.

Holding her hand, we get off the plane and are assaulted by the Ridgewood airport's air conditioning as we step into our gate.

"I'm so sorry." Declan rushes to us the second he sees us in baggage claim, pulling Sailor up into his arms. Her hand slips from mine as he hugs her tightly.

Pressing a kiss to the top of her head, he sets her back down and immediately pulls me into a tight hug, which surprises me, but is more than welcome. Wrapping my arms around him, I nuzzle my face against his chest and inhale his scent.

"It's not your fault." I let go of him and readjust my purse. "Thanks for picking us up."

"Of course." Declan's phone rings and he pulls it from his pocket, brows furrowing as he looks down at the screen. Ignoring the call, he shoves it back into his pants, then grabs Sailor's hand, and surprises me again when he reaches down to lace our fingers together too, like it's the most natural thing in the world. "Are you girls hungry? I brought snacks for the car, but dinner is ready at home."

Snacks and dinner made? Who is this man?

"I'm starving," Sailor whines, practically jogging next to her dad as he drags us both through the sea of people in the airport. It's not that he's walking fast necessarily, it's just that his legs are so much longer than both of ours that we are both having to keep up at a light trot.

The car ride seems to zip by quickly, the hour between Ridgewood and Bridge Point flying by in a blur as I sit in the front seat and try to keep myself from staring at Declan the whole time.

I'm not sure if our kiss has me seeing him in a whole new light, or if I'm really just *that* obsessed with him, but the attraction I've had for him feels more amplified than it has in previous days.

I'm falling for him fast. Which is ironic because I hate

reading insta-love in romance novels, but here I am, living my very own version. I guess to be fair, I've known Declan for a few months now, interacting on a daily basis and carrying out our very own forced, or at least close, proximity trope.

There's a nagging feeling in the back of my mind, though, nervous he's going to change his mind and want to go back to keeping things professional for the sake of Sailor. It's unsettling, but I push it to the back of my mind as he carries my suitcase up his walkway.

Stepping into the Lane house feels like coming home. The late evening sunlight pours into the open windows, draping the entryway and living room in a warm, golden glow. I drop my purse in its usual spot, and Sailor takes off running down the hallway toward her playroom with an excited squeal.

When we're alone, Declan bends down slightly, wrapping his strong arms around my waist. "Stay the night tonight." He scatters kisses across my neck, and I loop my arms around his.

I shiver in his embrace, pins and needles covering me from my head to my toes. "Are you sure that's a good idea?"

"I can't think of anything better except for maybe having a moment alone right now." His nose brushes against mine.

"Mmm," I hum. "That would be nice."

Our mouths meld together, falling back into a rhythm that's already becoming second nature, but within a few seconds, Sailor's footsteps pad down the hallway. Declan groans loudly as we pull away.

"Daddy, I'm hungry," she reminds him, rubbing her eyes as she comes into view. Poor girl is exhausted. She didn't nap at all on the plane, and it's been a long day.

"All right, princess, let's get some dinner in you. Early bedtime tonight." From over his shoulder, he winks at me, and that sweet feeling of anticipation trickles through my system.

As we walk into the kitchen, I hear the vibration of Declan's phone again. This time, though, he doesn't take it out of his pocket, and he simply squeezes the side of it through his pants, effectively silencing it.

With a fleeting look, he shrugs. "Addison."

Was she who called earlier, too? She's Sailor's mother. Of course she's going to reach out periodically. I know that.

But still, there's a worry I can't explain that takes root in the back of my mind, and dread forms a knot in my stomach that I promptly try to ignore.

Dinner is a delicious medley of roasted vegetables, paired with rosemary and parmesan chicken that he obviously went through a lot of trouble to make. There's a comfortable silence at the table when we all devour our food, the flavors exploding on my tongue with every bite.

I moan appreciatively—everything this man cooks is divine.

Beneath the table, Declan puts his hand on my thigh and squeezes tightly. He leans into me, and whispers, "Stop teasing me with your moans, sweetheart. I'm glad you like my cooking, but the only whimpers I want to hear from you are when my tongue is deep in your—"

"Daddy, I'm all done!" Sailor interrupts, shoving her plate away.

"Dammit," Declan mutters beneath his breath.

Sailor hops out of her chair. "I go play now?"

Laughing, I turn to the girl who just interrupted what could have been some intense blushing on my part.

"Alright, you can be excused," Declan tells her, and she runs off toward her playroom again.

He groans deeply again. "Is it bedtime yet?"

"You're the boss," I lift my shoulders in a playful way, "you tell me when to put her to sleep."

"The sooner the better." He glances at the clock on the stove. "I guess it's still kind of early.

I scoop the last bite of food into my mouth, chewing it quickly. When I'm finished, I drop my napkin next to the plate. "I'll go give her a bath. Leave the dishes in the sink, I'll do them when I finish with Sailor."

"No way. You don't have to do both."

"It's fine! You cooked. I don't mind."

"Hailey." His voice is firm. "You're not a housekeeper,

you're my..." he stops, hesitating. *I'm your what, Declan?* "I got the dishes, thank you for bathing Sailor."

My hand cups his cheek as I lean down to kiss him, wordlessly. When I walk away, he grabs my wrist and quickly pulls me backward. I land on his lap, and he buries his hand in my hair and kisses me harder.

Breathless, my lips feel swollen when he finally lets me go, and as I walk out of the room, I give a quick glance at the clock again.

One more hour until Sailor goes to bed and Declan and I can finally be alone.

"She's out," Declan lets me know as he joins me on the couch after tucking Sailor in for the night. It's been about thirty minutes since he went to her room, which tells me he was suckered into reading a few books before bed. He stifles a yawn and leans his head against the back of the couch, rolling it to face me.

"Declan, I've been thinking..." My thoughts trail off, stomach lurching as I swallow down the words I don't want to say.

Knitting his brows together, he stays silent, waiting for me to continue.

"I just want to make sure you're okay with this. On

some level, it's weird. We both know it's true. You hired me to be Sailor's nanny and now..."

"And now I can't imagine our lives without you, Hailey," he cuts me off. "You've become so much more than just Sailor's nanny. She loves you, and I love having you here with us." Playing with my hair, he scoots closer on the couch, then brings his other hand to grip my chin, tilting my head in his direction. "I have no doubt in my mind that I want to see where this can go between us. I know the risks, and I'd be lying if I said the thought of potentially losing you, not just for my own selfish reasons, but for Sailor, is absolutely terrifying, but not enough to keep me from you."

He kisses me softly, pulling me in with his heartfelt words and gentle touch. A sigh of relief pours out of me as Declan whispers, "Let me take you to bed, sweetheart. It's about time I show you just how much I appreciate all you do for this family."

Standing, he takes my hand and pulls me to my feet. Our fingers tangle as he leads me from the living room, taking me to a space that I've felt was off-limits up until now.

When we enter his room, I'm hit with Declan's scent. It washes over me, calming my nerves while setting my soul on fire. This is happening. It's *really* happening.

I walk in further, looking around at his dark walls and hunter green bedding. There are photos on the wall, framed around the flatscreen TV hanging across from his bed. A simple dresser sits next to the wall, and there's an attached bathroom. The room is spacious and minimally furnished, but cozy and incredibly *him*.

As I take it all in, I hear the door shut behind me. A smile pulls at my lips when Declan comes up behind me and sweeps my hair off my neck before he presses his lips to the delicate skin.

"Are you sure you want this, sweetheart? It's not too late to say no."

More than I want my next breath, Declan.

But I say nothing and turn to face him. Sliding my hands up his chest, I encircle his neck with my arms, resting them loosely on his shoulders, then push up on my tiptoes and kiss him.

It quickly erupts into more—our hands wander, our tongues tangle.

Declan's capable hands grip the hemline of my shirt, pulling it over my head with urgency. I do the same to his, grabbing a handful of fabric and pull it up. He helps remove it, and tosses it to the side.

Next goes my bra, and as he unhooks it, a different kind of satisfaction sparks. I tip my head back as one of Declan's palms grips my breast, and the heat of his tongue slides from my clavicle to my jaw.

Reaching down, I rub his erection through his jeans, feeling how hard and incredibly huge he is, and it dawns on me that it might not fit inside of me. It's daunting, but it doesn't stop me from unhooking the button on his pants and rolling down the zipper.

Declan sucks in a sharp breath and thrusts into my palm when I wrap my fingers around him. "*Fuck,* sweetheart."

"You might be too big," I breathe, stroking his shaft with one hand while I use the other to start pushing down his jeans and underwear. It's not the most eloquent of movements, but it's getting the job done.

"It'll fit, don't worry." He pushes his clothes down the rest of the way until he's completely nude in front of me, and I'm naked from the waist up.

I take a minute to admire him—the ridges of his abs, the sexy Adonis belt that is practically an arrow leading to his erection that juts out, thick and commanding. Finally, I graze my eyes up his body and connect with his. They shine with desire as he looks back at me, and he takes a step forward, his hands tugging on the waist of my jeans. Undoing them, he silently pushes them down, taking my panties with them, until they pool at my feet. He doesn't give me the chance to step out of them before I'm lifted into his arms and walked to his bed.

He lays me against the mattress with ease, taking his time to gently place me down. "You're so damn beautiful, Hailey." He kisses my shoulder. "Inside." The top of my breast. "And out." He takes my nipple into his mouth, swirling the sensitive peak around on his tongue before releasing it. "I love your body." A gentle kiss is placed on my stomach. "Every inch of you is perfect."

"I have my flaws," I tell him, insecurity rearing its ugly head without warning.

"Not to me."

I gasp when his fingers touch my center, spreading me without hesitation, like he's already well acquainted with my body.

My legs fall open when he starts to strum his fingertips against my clit like it's his own personal instrument—and maybe it is, since a chorus of moans falls from my lips. Closing my eyes, I do everything in my power to let go of everything other than *this* feeling.

This *incredible* feeling.

"I'm going to start stretching you a little, sweetheart. Get you ready for me." His voice is gruff and strained, like he's holding back from his own pleasure to create mine.

"Let me touch you." I reach for him, but he pulls his hips away.

"Hailey, the only action I've gotten in the last two years is by my own hand, aside from the other night with you. If you touch me, I can't guarantee I won't come in yours the moment you stroke me. Right now, I want to make you feel good, sweetheart. Can you let me do that for you?"

Not waiting for a response, he pushes a finger into me.

"Oh my God," I cry out, bucking my hips.

"That's my girl," Declan growls in my ear before nibbling on the lobe. "I think you can handle another, what do you think?"

"Yes," I moan as he slowly adds a second.

Pumping his fingers, the sound of my arousal is audible as he glides them in and out of me, changing angles and stroking me from inside. Scooping some of the wetness, he smears it all over, making me slippery.

A flicker of embarrassment hits me from how wet I am —have I ever been this aroused for a man before?

I don't think so. But Declan isn't just any man. He's different.

My body feels it.

My heart does too.

His thumb strokes against my clit, and I buck my hips again, my back arching against the bed. He takes his time, rubbing and stroking, before I feel the tip of another finger at my entrance, ready to join the other two. "I think you're ready for another."

A statement. Not a question.

I can't help but hold my breath a little as he starts pushing in a third finger. It's more than I've ever taken in the past, and I'm nervous it'll be uncomfortable, but I quickly shove those thoughts aside as Declan moves his mouth to my breast and takes my nipple into his mouth again. The sensation, hot and wet against my skin, pulls the focus from the slight discomfort of being stretched more than I have before.

I don't tell him that I've only been with one other man before, and that he was a two-pump chump who didn't care to even attempt to make me come. I gave him the benefit of the doubt a few times before calling it a learning experience and swearing off men to focus on *me*.

So, yeah, you could call me inexperienced—but Declan's doing a stellar job at putting my mind and body at ease.

Sucking in a breath, I feel my core flutter.

Declan rewards me with a moan. "You're doing so well for me, sweetheart. Letting me handle your body how I want...fingering you like this...stretching this pretty pussy just for me."

My eyes roll back, his words fueling my arousal even more than I thought possible.

"Did you know you have a praise kink, Hailey?" he asks curiously, slowly thrusting his fingers inside of me, hitting a new angle that makes my toes curl.

I shake my head. "No."

"So my good girl has only just learned she likes to be praised? Lucky me for being the man to figure it out."

"Declan," I moan again, my hips now mirroring his fingers. I want more of him—all of him. "Please."

"You're doing so good for me, sweetheart. Do you want more?"

"Yes. *Yes.*" I grip onto his duvet, bunching the blanket in my fists.

Declan groans, and slowly withdraws his fingers, using my arousal to coat his cock before scooping more from my body, and adding it onto his. My cheeks heat again when I see how his shaft glistens from *me.*

"Don't you dare be embarrassed," he scolds. "This is the sexiest fucking thing I've ever seen."

Shifting onto his knees, he grabs my hips and pulls me to him, angling me exactly how he wants me.

Holding himself at the root, he aligns his cock with my entrance, then hesitates. His brows knit together as he looks down at us. "I should have been a gentleman, or at least a decent fucking human, and asked if I could fuck you bare..."

Oh. Oh shit.

Fuck. I'm too turned on to give a shit—consequences be damned. He just told me he hasn't been with anyone in years, and neither have I.

Lifting my hips, I press into him. "I want to feel you, Declan. All of you."

"Fuck, you're so perfect." He presses into me an inch, and I cry out from the sudden pressure.

He's way too big—I can't...I can't...

"Breathe for me, sweetheart."

A stream of air passes through my lips.

He pushes in a little more. "Such a good fucking girl."

Declan's thumb finds my clit again, circling it with an expertise of my body that didn't take him long to learn.

His hips roll a little, driving him in more. "Breathe."

"You're so fucking big, Declan," I exhale shakily.

He laughs, dropping his head against my shoulder. "And you're so damn tight I might come before I even get all the way inside of you."

"Push all the way," I tell him, clutching onto his shoulders.

"I don't want to hurt you," he argues.

"Do it, Declan. And kiss me."

Smashing our lips together, our tongues find each other and he deepens the kiss before his hips give one final thrust until he's sheathed inside me.

For several seconds, he doesn't move, and I'm able to adjust. Then, in the blink of an eye, my body combusts as I turn desperate for more.

"Move," I demand into his kiss, and he wastes no time before starting to rock into me.

Pushing my hair away from my face, Declan grips my jaw as he continues to kiss me, our bodies coming together over and over again.

My moans mix with his, our skin slapping together with every movement. He feels like heaven, and home, and everything I didn't know I was missing up until this exact moment—something so carnal and precious I wonder how I ever went without this level of intimacy before.

"Hailey, I can't last, sweetheart. You—" he groans mid-sentence, unable to control his pleasure. "Do you want me to stop?"

"No!" I cry, because it's possible I might actually perish if he stops.

"Fuck—I can't—" And then he roars with his release, his hips moving erratically as he spills himself inside of me. My body is wound so tight I'm surprised I don't topple over the edge with him, but I'm right there—so close, yet so far.

That's okay, I think to myself, expecting him to pull out of me, roll over, and be ready for bed. *Next time.*

Declan shudders, still riding the high of his climax, when he roughly pulls himself out of me. Tossing me around like a rag doll, cum still drips from his semi-erect cock as he scurries down the bed and climbs between my legs.

"What are yo—" a scream erupts from me as Declan sucks my clit into his mouth, rolling the tip of his tongue around the sensitive nerve.

My vision darkens, hands flying to the back of his head, as he suctions around it and thrusts two fingers into me.

I barely register the noises I make, not entirely sure they're human, as I come harder than I ever have in my life. It's like I'm floating above my body, the orgasm rolling into me as relentlessly as Declan's tongue.

I'm quaking by the time he kisses up my body and collapses on the blankets next to me. I can't even open my eyes, completely spent and satiated.

"That was...amazing."

"You're okay? That wasn't too much? I wanted to be more gentle, but goddamn..." Concern flickers through his features, and I roll over to face him.

Cupping my hand against his cheek, I shake my head. "It was incredible."

"You're incredible." He kisses the tip of my nose.

Contentment settles around us as we lie next to each other, tracing patterns on each other's skin. I draw a heart, and he writes his name, and it's so innocent and pure it nearly takes my breath away.

How is this real life? *My* life, no less.

After a while, the cold gets to me and I shiver, despite the body heat he radiates.

"Should we go get cleaned up?" I ask, rolling onto my back in preparation of getting up.

But Declan scoffs, grabbing me by the waist and pulling me against his body. Slowly, he shakes his head and walks his fingers down to the short curls above the apex of my thighs. "Fuck no, sweetheart. We've got all night."

CHAPTER NINETEEN

Declan

I'm startled awake, a sheen of sweat layering over my skin as I sit up in bed. The room is dark, but Hailey's fire-hued hair is fanned out over the pillow on what I'm hoping to permanently call her side of the bed.

The sight of her comforts me, even while in a state of fear. I can't remember the dream, but I know the way it made me feel.

Uneasy.

Inadequate.

Like disaster is looming just off in the distance.

Quietly, I toss my legs over the edge of the bed, rubbing my hand down my face. I need a cold bottle of water to ease the edge, then I'll go back to bed.

The flooring is cool on my feet as I enter the kitchen, squinting as I pull open the fridge and am assaulted by the light. Chugging down one of the cold bottles of water, I crumple it and toss it into the nearby trash can before I head back upstairs.

Entering the room, I'm ready to crawl back under the sheets. I push back the covers, stopping for a minute to look down at the woman sleeping contentedly.

It's crazy to me that less than six months ago, she wasn't in my life at all, and now, in the span of the last few weeks, so much has changed between us.

It's hard to pinpoint a time frame where my view of her shifted from just being Sailor's nanny into realizing my attraction to her was more than just a physical one, but I think it happened much earlier than I care to admit.

The only thing that's been standing in my way is myself. Even though I'm terrified that if I were to lose Hailey, Sailor would inevitably lose her too. I still feel this is a necessary risk for both of us.

Hailey is everything I've ever wanted—ever hoped for. She's not only perfect for me, but perfect for Sailor, too. She's proven time and time again just how much she loves my daughter. Not because she has to, but because she wants to. I never once fathomed that a woman stepping into our home to become our nanny would be capable of such an incredible maternal relationship with my daughter, but then again, there's no one else in the world like Hailey Shea.

Slipping into the bed beside her, the mattress dips from my weight, and I scoot closer, tucking my arm around her midsection. She grumbles in her sleep as I pull her tight against me, but snuggles into my chest further, fitting against my body in the perfect little spoon.

The feel of her skin against mine instantly makes me hard, images of her writhing beneath me earlier flash through my mind, and the contentment I went to bed with reignites into desperation.

Gliding the back of my hand down the side of her breast, my fingertips trace over her stomach, pausing briefly at the waistband of her cotton underwear before I easily move them aside.

Spreading her lips, I find her clit and start tracing small circular motions with my middle finger. I toy with it lazily until she starts to rock her hips in her sleep, unknowing where the pleasure is coming from, only recognizing that her body should be chasing it.

I strum my fingers against her center, pulling up the wetness she's leaking until it coats her sensitive bundle, and I intensify my ministrations.

She moans, pressing her ass back against my dick, and seconds later sucks in a sharp breath when I press a finger inside of her.

"Declan," she moans, my name like a prayer on the tip of her tongue.

My lips trace the shell of her ear. "Shhh. You're such a good girl, sweetheart. Your body is so wet and ready for me already, even when you're asleep. Is this what I have to look forward to night after night?"

She hums in agreement, pressing against me more. "Keep going," she whimpers.

My finger never strays from her clit. "This pussy is so wet, I could have slid right inside you and fucked you while you slept. Would you like that, sweetheart? To wake up with me inside you?"

"Yes," she moans. "More."

"Or maybe we'll just go to sleep tonight with my dick in your heat. Warming it, keeping it cozy all. Night. Long." I enunciate every word, pride blooming in my chest at how with each sentence that comes out of my mouth, Hailey grows wetter. "You're such a good girl, you'd let me do that, wouldn't you? Make us both feel good."

"My God, Declan, please. I need you," she pleads. "I need you inside me."

"*Fuck*, sweetheart. How can I deny you when you beg so beautifully?"

Shoving her panties down, I push my sweatpants down, too, and let my dick spring free. Hitching her leg up over mine, I spread her, sliding the tip in her arousal to lubricate it.

She's making a mess out of me as I glide my shaft from her tight pussy to her ass. "You're so fucking wet, Hailey, I don't even need extra lubricant to get you ready. Already so fucking drenched for me."

The head of my dick rubs against her, and I wish I could see the pleasure on her face, but the anticipation of fucking her from behind has my balls tightening prematurely.

Feeling like I'm in danger of coming without even putting it in, I reach over her hip, my fingers diving between her legs to play with her clit more, winding her up because I know this won't last as long as I'd like it to.

She makes me feral, unable to stop myself from getting off the moment I'm inside her.

Holding my dick at the base, I align myself, lifting her leg higher as I push inside, groaning in pleasure as she cries out.

"Fuck! Oh my God, Declan!"

Her cunt is impossibly tight from this angle, and I have to squeeze my eyes shut to stop from coming. "Dig your nails into my leg, sweetheart."

"What?" she asks, breathless and confused.

"You feel too fucking good. Dig your nails into my leg."

She does, and the bite of her fingernails is enough to hold me off. "Goddammit," I curse.

"I need you to move, Declan. Fuck me, *please*."

So for the third time tonight, I oblige what my girl wants and I rock my hips.

"Where are we going?" Hailey's contagious laughter bubbles through my car as we drive away from the house, her vision eliminated by the black silk scarf covering her eyes.

It's been a week since the day everything changed between us, and I have no idea how I convinced myself for so long that she wasn't everything I wanted. It's been a long few days, and last night I decided I couldn't wait any longer to take her out.

After making a quick, last-minute phone call with the promise of a fully paid-for round-trip ticket, dinner delivery, and a place to stay, Hartley agreed to fly up for the night to watch Sailor so I could take her sister on a proper date.

Money well spent, in my opinion.

"You'll see," I tease, squeezing her thigh.

She looks amazing in a hunter green mini dress that hugs every single one of her curves. She almost changed out of it, but I convinced her not to when I slid my hand up her thigh and whispered a few pretty words while I made her feel good.

I thought nothing was sexier than when she came, but then I got to witness it in the mirror, while she was fully clothed, after watching my fingers thrust relentlessly under her dress.

Fuck, that will forever be ingrained in my mind.

"Can I have a hint?" The playfulness in her tone matches the smile on her face.

"We have a twenty minute drive."

"That's the worst hint ever." She laughs. "Give me another?"

"You're overdressed."

"Declan!" she squeals. "I told you to let me change!"

"Not a chance, sweetheart." My fingers dig deeper into her thigh. "This dress is like a slow torture that'll keep my dick hard all night."

"You're killing me."

"Not as much as it's going to kill me not to sink into you the second we're out of this car."

She laughs again before changing the subject.

Our conversation flows easily as we spend the next several minutes traveling out of Bridge Point and into the countryside of Deerbrook Valley, where Gareth Fox's family owns a picturesque lakeside ranch.

Wanting a unique place for our first official date, I called in a favor.

She has no idea I have a full picnic dinner in the trunk, or that Hartley packed an overnight bag for her, just in case we decide to stay in the guest cabin instead of going home.

The road turns from smooth asphalt to bumpy gravel as I turn down the unmarked road. Up ahead, an archway with a sign reading Fox Den Ranch acts as a beacon on where to go.

"Maybe I've watched too many true crime shows, but is this the part where you murder me, Declan?" Hailey asks, her fingers floating up to the blindfold, preparing to lift it.

"We're almost there, keep that on." I touch her gently, lacing our fingers together before I bring the back of her hand to my lips.

"Okay." Her voice is small, but she bites her lip, suppressing a smile.

When I pull my car off to the side of the lake, the sun's beginning its descent to the horizon. The timing couldn't be more perfect.

Hopping out, I pop the trunk before walking around to Hailey's side and opening the door. I grab her hand and help her out, then guide her with my palm against the small of her back.

We walk down to the dock, where two wooden rocking chairs wait for us.

Before I lift her blindfold, I kiss her deeply. She sighs in contentment, then I take a step back.

Lifting the black silk from her eyes, I watch as they light up while she takes in her surroundings. "Where are we?" she asks in wonder.

"Fox Den Ranch. The Fox family owns it."

She's quiet as she takes in our surroundings, and for some reason, that makes me a little unsure I made the right decision in bringing her here for our first outing alone. "I know it's not the traditional dinner and a movie—"

"It's perfect," she cuts me off. Turning toward me, she wraps her arms around my middle. "Have you heard of the love languages?"

My brows raise to my forehead. "Uh, I don't think so?"

"There are five love languages, and each individual person tends to favor one or two. Words of affirmation, physical touch, acts of service, receiving gifts, and quality time."

"Your love language is words of affirmation."

Hailey tosses her head back and laughs. "I think that's only with *you*, but yes, that's a newly discovered love language. Quality time has always been my number one."

I tighten my hold on her waist, then kiss her cheek. "Then I guess I planned a pretty good first date after all. Because it's just you, me, and the lake for the rest of the night."

"I love that." She beams, and it's prettier than the rays of the golden hour sun reflecting off the lake.

I leave her standing on the dock and go back to the car to grab the supplies out of the trunk. After setting up the picnic blanket near the side of the lake, I pull out the cooler I packed and begin arranging our food options—a charcuterie board I put together, since she liked the last one I made so much, and a few drink options, not knowing what she's in the mood for.

When she joins me, she finds a seat on the blanket, then nudges my backpack with her foot. "You really do bring this thing everywhere you go."

"A guy has to have some way to cart all his crap around. This time it's packed with your stuff, though." I start making her a plate, putting a little bit of everything on it.

"My stuff?" she questions as I pass it to her.

"Yeah." I grin, picking up a plate for myself. "Rented the guest house for the night, so if you decide we should stay, we'll stay. But if you'd like to go back, we can do that instead. Or if you get cold, you have a change of clothes."

"You thought of all that for me?" Hailey looks stunned, and it makes me wonder something.

"I thought of all that for purely selfish reasons. Has a man ever taken you on a getaway, sweetheart?"

Her eyes widen for a second before she looks down at the plate in her hands. "Nope. Never."

The familiar feeling of possessiveness sparks within me. "Lucky me. I get to be the one who shows you how a real man treats a woman."

I don't ask Hailey for more details about her past relationships. Frankly, they don't matter one iota to me because after just one week of intimacy with this woman, I can tell you there's no way in hell I'm ever letting her go.

Thoughts of fear and uncertainty went out the window by day three. She's what I want for both me *and* Sailor.

And I'll take things at whatever pace she wants to go at, so long as I don't have to ever give her up.

She thinks about what I said for a minute before a mischievous smile blooms across her face. Setting her plate down, she pushes up to her knees and faces me. "Oh, yeah?" she taunts. "But what if I want to show you how a woman treats a man?"

Her hands move to my belt and she looks up at me from under her lashes, and I know in that moment I'm well and truly fucked.

There's no way I'm not falling for her at a much faster rate than what's probably acceptable, but apparently that saying rings true: when you know, you know.

Grabbing her backside in both hands, I yank her toward me, forcing her to collapse onto me, and we roll backward, my back hitting the blanket on top of the soft earth. Her hair floats down around us, her eyes burning with desire.

Before I pull her to me for a kiss, I state with certainty, "Then I guess we'll both have a very happy life together, sweetheart."

CHAPTER TWENTY

"So how was it?" Hartley asks over her steaming mug of coffee the second Declan shuts the door behind him as he leaves for work.

We got back from Fox Den Ranch early this morning, trying to beat the morning commuter traffic. Declan needed to get to the stadium before noon, anyway.

My eyes meet my sister's from across the island. Leaning against it with my mug in my hands, all I can do is bite my lip. I know I'm blushing—*as usual*—I can feel the heat of it.

"Hailey Nicolette Shea. Tell me *everything*."

So I do. I tell her about the drive and the picnic. Watching the sunset while we lay in each other's arms. Skinny dipping in the moonlight. Our skin covered in gooseflesh after we got out of the water. The body heat we utilized to warm up.

I spare no detail for my sister, and after I'm done, I definitely feel like I overshared.

With her jaw slackened, Hartley stares at me for a few minutes, wide-eyed. Then, she gives a frustrated sigh. "I need a new man."

"Break up with Owen," I volley immediately. I'm not a fan of the smug bastard who treats my sister like shit half the time.

"It's not that simple," she argues. I narrow my eyes, judging her because, as her sister, I'm allowed to.

I'm not sure what's not simple about it, but I won't press further. Instead, I ask, "What time do you want me to drop you off at the airport?"

The thought of her going home so soon makes me sad, but I'm grateful that she took the time to make this quick trip happen. Declan doesn't have many options when it comes to help with Sailor, so when he wanted to get a babysitter so we could go out, he was at a complete loss.

"Maybe in about an hour and a half?" She shrugs, then takes a sip of her coffee.

"Alright." I set my mug down after chugging the rest of the lukewarm drink. "Let me get Sailor ready, then. It takes about an hour to get to the airport from here, so we should get on the road soon."

"Okay, *good girl*, whatever you want." Hartley leans her elbow on the counter and places her chin in the palm of her hand, batting her eyelashes at me.

I'll regret telling her about discovering how much praise turns me on for the rest of my life.

Tossing a crumpled up paper towel across the island, I flip her the bird.

"Love you, sissy!" she calls out to me, laughing as I walk away.

Our airport goodbye is full of tears and several warm hugs, with promises of seeing each other soon. Hartley promise's she'll be back before turning to walk through the automatic doors that lead into the airport.

It hurts watching her go, and by the sad look on Sailor's face, I know I'm not the only one who wants her to stay.

Seeing Hartley twice in the span of a week renewed a joy within me I'd been missing, but I desperately wish my sister would just move to Bridge Point.

As it is now, I don't see myself moving down south again—certainly not at the rate things are progressing with me and Declan.

One thing I *didn't* confide in Hartley about, though, was *that* conversation.

Our future.

Such a heavy topic for a new relationship, but with a child involved, it was necessary.

We talked about her, both of us realizing we have the same fear of hurting her if things between us don't work out.

Not only is Sailor's well-being common ground, but it's a priority for both of us.

I could see the relief in his eyes when he realized I care just as much about how this will affect her as he does.

But that conversation also made things feel exponentially more real.

I also expressed my need to finish college before things get too serious between us, and he told me I am in the driver's seat. We can progress our relationship as slowly or as quickly as I want.

He isn't going anywhere.

Which is reassuring, but that little voice in the back of my head still is telling me to proceed with caution.

And now, as I drive back to his home in Bridge Point, every mile feels uncertain.

Something is wrong.

Off.

I can feel it in every inch of my body.

Glancing in the rearview mirror, Sailor's neck hangs in an incredibly uncomfortable position as she sleeps in her car seat.

Lovely. Now she won't sleep when we get home, and she'll be an emotional rollercoaster by dinner.

A pop music station plays on the radio, doing its job of keeping me focused with upbeat liveliness while I continue down the road. The drive from Ridgewood to Bridge Point is monotonous. I start thinking about yesterday, and I'm hit with a wave of longing.

I miss him.

Using the automated feature on my car's dashboard, I call Declan. He might still be coaching, but I want to hear his voice.

He answers on the second ring, his deep timbre filling my car speakers. "Hey, sweetheart."

"Hey," I drawl. "Bad time?"

From the speaker, the distinguishable sound of a ball connects with a bat, then some muffling directly on the phone, like he's moving away for some privacy.

"Not at all. Everything okay?"

"Yeah, everything's good. I just dropped Hartley off at the airport. Sailor fell asleep in the back, so I was hoping for a little company. But I can hear you're still at work, so I won't keep you."

"I'm hoping to be out of here soon. How about I fire up the grill when I get home and make us some barbecue chicken sandwiches as an early dinner?"

"Oh gosh, Sailor would love that. She's been asking to go to Chick-fil-A all day."

Declan laughs. "Well, not much tops Chick-fil-A, but I think my sandwiches are a pretty close second."

"Hmm. I'll be the judge of that," I tease, my stomach already growling. I guarantee they'll be better than the popular fast food chains and I'm a stan for them.

"I look forward to your critique," Declan muses.

Smiling, I drum my fingers against the steering wheel and sit up a little straighter in my seat. "I'll let you go, see you shortly?"

"Hopefully within the next forty-five."

It'll be longer than that, I'm sure. It always is with that unruly bunch of Bears.

"Perfect, see you then."

Declan says goodbye, and I jab my finger into the screen on the dashboard to hang up, feeling much more at ease.

At least for a moment.

When I turn onto Declan's street, the dread hits me like a brick to the stomach.

I can't explain the feeling—everything looks normal. Everything *is* normal.

Sailor wakes up when I pull Declan's car into the garage, already cranky from the crooked-neck catnap. Walking around to her side, I take her out of her car seat, and she goes limp in my arms, her head resting against my shoulder.

The garage closes behind me, and as I go through the

door leading into the house, I immediately catch the scent of a perfume I don't recognize.

My stomach drops, and I realize I'm not alone.

Startled, I jump back and cradle Sailor tighter in my arms, staring at the woman sitting at the kitchen table, looking down at her phone.

Her dark hair drapes over the side of her face, but it only takes about fifteen seconds for me to recognize her. "Addison?"

Her attention snaps to me, and she places her phone face down on the kitchen table, plastering a saccharine smile on her perfectly made up face. "Oh! You must be the new nanny. Hi, I'm Sailor's mom."

Really bold of you to assume you're a mother when you've been absent for the last two years, but okay, I think to myself, but don't dare voice it aloud.

Standing, she takes a step toward us, and instinctively, I take a small step back. "Sailor! My love, come see Mommy." She speaks to her in a baby voice, and Sailor lifts her head, looking over at her mother.

I'm not all that surprised when she *doesn't* make any attempt to wiggle out of my arms.

Visibly annoyed, Addison crosses the kitchen with her arms out like she's about ready to grab her from me.

Protectiveness rears its head despite this woman being Sailor's mother, and I pivot so she can't pull her from my arms. "Sailor just woke up from a nap in the car. She's not quite awake yet."

I smile, but anger flashes through Addison's eyes as she watches me with her child.

It feels wrong not to immediately oblige and reunite her with her daughter, but Declan would have told me if he'd known she was going to be here. He wouldn't have let me walk into this blindly.

Sailor doesn't even know her. She was a baby when she left.

"Give me my daughter," Addison demands. She leaves no room for me to object and pulls Sailor from my arms, despite the tight hold I have on her.

Sailor immediately starts crying.

Anger turns into shock as she tries to console her. "Why are you crying, baby?" she coos. "Mommy has you."

Addison starts bouncing as if she's trying to comfort a newborn, and it takes everything in me to keep my mouth shut.

I'm at a complete loss for what to even say to her. Questions race through my mind, and I realize I should probably dig my phone out of my purse to call Declan, but the thoughts don't fully register for me enough to actually do it.

Why is she here?
How did she get in?
Does she still have a key?

"Put me down!" Sailor whines, squirming in her mother's grasp.

Being much bigger than she was when Addison left, Sailor is able to break free from her hold, and Addison's forced to put her down, otherwise she will drop her.

The second her feet touch the floor, Sailor runs back to me, her arms wrapping around my leg as she steps behind me. Addison plasters a fake smile onto her face and smooths her blouse, but the look of fury is undeniable.

In a sickeningly sweet voice, she bends and addresses Sailor. "That's okay, baby. You'll remember me after we spend a few days together."

A few days? Does Declan know she's here?

"Does Declan know you're here?" I verbalize my thoughts.

Her eyes narrow just a beat before she shakes her head. "Oh, no! I'm going to surprise Decky! I can't wait to see the look on his face when he gets home from work. He'll be so excited to see I'm back—I've been away from home for far too long."

Decky? Away from home?

Alarm bells ring in my direction. She doesn't outwardly say it, but with the way she's speaking to me, I know she knows him and I are together.

Her smile is all teeth before her eyes travel down my body, fully and openly judging me. There's a slight roll of her eyes before she jets her hand out, opening and closing it a couple of times in Sailor's direction.

"Do you want to show Mommy your playroom?" Then, dramatically, she gasps. "Oh my gosh, Sai Sai. I forgot, I have a present for you!"

Practically gliding over to the table, she reaches for a small package wrapped in silver gift wrap, with an extravagant matching bow on top.

Sailor perks up at the word *present*, curiously breaking away from me to go take it from Addison's hands.

In true kid fashion, she obliterates the wrapping paper, tossing it to the floor before she rips open the box. Inside is a bright pink device that looks like a miniature cell phone.

"What is that?" I blurt, unable to contain my immediate irritation.

Addison eyes me like I'm the dumbest person in the world. Her tone reflects that, too. "You haven't seen the KidzCall3? It's the top-of-the-line kid's cell phone on the market right now!" There's a hint of pride in her voice, and I wonder what level of delusion this woman is.

"She's three," I spit, my tone leaving no room for friendly banter or any sort of cordialness. I'm at a loss for words, completely flabbergasted by the woman in front of me. The educator in me immediately makes a mental list of the reasons why this is the worst idea on the planet.

"That's why it's only programmed to call me, and her

father," Addison tells me, annunciating like she's speaking a language I don't understand.

My mouth opens and closes like a fish out of water, trying to formulate a response. This woman really just shows up out of nowhere and gives her three-year-old a phone so she can call her.

Sailor looks just as confused as I am, inspecting the pink gadget for a moment before losing all interest and setting it on the floor.

Addison scoffs and bends to pick it up, putting it on the table instead. Then reaches for Sailor's hand, not giving her the option of refusing to hold it. "Are you ready to show Mommy your playroom now, sweetheart? I can't wait to see all your new toys."

I flinch at the term of endearment, the nickname coming from her mouth immediately making me want to burst into tears.

Watching me through narrow eyes, Addison leads Sailor out of the kitchen, the click of her heels that she didn't bother taking off growing fainter as they disappear down the hallway together.

And I'm left standing here wondering what the hell is going on, and is everything about to fall apart?

CHAPTER TWENTY-ONE

Declan

GARETH FOX

I hate to be the bearer of bad news, but one of the kiss videos has nineteen million views.

AUSTIN COOPER

How is that bad? We're selling out games, baby!

GARETH FOX

It's bad because that's Coach's private moment broadcasted for the entire world to see.

JENSEN FIELDS JR.

Not to be a dick, but maybe he shouldn't have kissed her so openly then. Or, million dollar thought, maybe he doesn't care and you're making a mountain out of a molehill.

AUSTIN COOPER

You're always a dick, Jensen.

JENSEN FIELDS JR.

You wouldn't like me if I was nice.

AUSTIN COOPER

I'd like you more than I like you now.

GARETH FOX

Do you possess that quality?

JENSEN FIELDS JR.

You like me plenty, it's why you try to pick fights with me like we're an old married couple.

AUSTIN COOPER

You'd be so lucky to have me as a husband.

JENSEN FIELDS JR.

Who said you'd be the husband?

GARETH FOX

Stop acting like teenagers.

GARETH FOX

Your boss is in this chat, or have you forgotten?

AUSTIN COOPER

Is Coach technically our boss?

GARETH FOX

YES.

"Oh, God," I groan, pinching the bridge of my nose as I toss my phone into the passenger seat.

It's been a long fucking day and these three are grating on my nerves. Everything is grating on my nerves actually, including a certain mother of my child, if you can even call her a mother.

Addison's called three more times over the course of the last five days, and ironically, when I finally have the energy to deal with her, she doesn't answer the phone. This is the most she has ever called in a short span, and it's really fucking irritating me. I'm not naive enough to believe she wants to speak to Sailor.

No, she probably saw those damn videos online.

Sitting in my driveway, I let the air conditioner run, taking a few minutes to myself and listening to an old AC/DC song. The cool air blows in my face, calming my nerves a bit.

It's a start, anyway. It's been less than a week since we've been back in town after the game against the Rebels, and so much has changed. Not only with our relationship, but my outlook on life.

I've spent so much time and energy worrying about everyone else, that I've forgotten to make myself happy in the process.

Hailey's reshaped the way I prioritize my life.

Of course, Sailor is, and will always be, my number

one priority, but for once in my life, baseball isn't the second.

I love having Hailey around. In my home. In my bed. Sneaking her in and out so Sailor doesn't notice has made me feel like a teenager again, and the lightweight, giddy feeling that comes along with it is one I've missed.

But last week was just the tip of the iceberg with my time management struggles. As games ramp up, so will my schedule, and I'll have to re-evaluate how much extra time is spent on the field after what's truly needed, so I can make sure I'm staying attentive to both of my girls.

That starts today.

I needed to go to the stadium for four hours, and as soon as practice was finished, I was out of there.

I held myself to it, too.

It feels good—really good.

And I can't wait to spend the rest of my evening at home barbecuing, relaxing, and being with the two people in my life who shine the brightest.

Killing the engine of my truck, I hop out, keeping the keys in my hand as I stride up the walkway. There's a pep in my step, a song from earlier on the radio stuck in my head that I sing under my breath while unlocking the door.

As soon as I push it open, though, my smile drops. Two things happen at once. First, the stomach-churning familiarity of Addison's perfume pummels me square in the face, and second, I see a very expensive, very ostentatious purse sitting on my entryway table that I know for certain isn't Hailey's.

A string of curses fly from my mouth as I barrel through my house, looking for whoever I come across first. My first stop is Sailor's playroom, which is exactly where I find my daughter and ex-fiancée playing tea party.

"Daddy!" Sailor shouts when she sees me, flying up from her chair so she can run to me. I catch her, bringing her in for a hug while staring daggers at her mother across the room.

"Hi, Sail. Did you have a fun day today?"

"Hailey took me to the airport!" she tells me proudly.

I kiss her cheek. "I know she did. That's so cool."

I find it very telling that Sailor doesn't mention anything about her mom, them playing, or her being here. Jesus, does Sailor even remember who Addison is? She was a baby when she walked out.

Putting her down, I step closer to my ex, who's now standing just a few feet away with a plastic smile I've come to realize is as fake as her breasts. "What are you doing here, Addison?"

"Hey, Decky. Miss me?" She bats her eyelashes, which I'm ashamed to say used to work.

"No," I deadpan. "What do you want?"

Sailor leaves my side and goes to play with her Barbies, which thankfully are across the room. I don't want to have this conversation in front of her. Hell, I don't want to have it at all but here we are.

"Can't a woman miss her family?" Addison lays on a seduction attempt thick, trailing her fingers from my pec to my shoulder. I shrug her off. "You look good, Declan. Fatherhood agrees with you."

Laughter erupts from me—a mixture of frustration and exasperation. Grinding my teeth, I respond in a gritty whisper, "You have some nerve."

"I want you back, Declan. I want us to be together, and to raise our daughter—"

"The fact—" I yell, then remind myself I need to lower my voice, not wanting to sway Sailor's attention. "The fact that you even just referred to Sailor as your daughter is absurd. You walked out on us when she was barely walking. You chose an attempt at a career over your own child."

"She *is* my daughter, Declan. Whether you like it or not. You, me, and her—we're a family. We can be one again."

"Absolutely not, Addison. You lost that chance when you walked out the door. Now tell me what you're really doing here because I don't buy the 'I want my family back' bullshit you're spewing."

"You've always thought the worst of me." She crosses her arms over her chest, glaring at me.

My eyes narrow into slits. "Only when you've shown your true colors."

"I have a right to see my daughter."

"Yeah, you do. But I have a right to tell you to get the fuck out of my house, too."

"You can't stop me from seeing her, Declan."

"Then take me to court, Addison. Get a visitation schedule put in place. But don't you dare show up to my home under the guise of wanting to get back together."

"*Our* home." She put her hands on her hips. "This is *our* home."

My jaw clenches. She knows damn well I owned this house before I even met her. She has no legal entitlement to it—we were never married.

"Fine, Declan!" she seethes. "You're not interested in getting back together with me? Then whatever. But I know that red headed floozy has been warming your bed at night, and playing mommy to my kid."

"What did you expect me to do? Not hire a nanny? Not move on? Life didn't stop just because you picked up and moved to Hollywood. I figured it the fuck out."

"I think you forgot that I carried Sailor for nine months. *I* went through twenty-seven hours of labor with her. Not you. Yes, I may have taken a path where I chose myself instead of motherhood, but I had my reasons for doing that, and I guarantee they're not at all what you expect them to be. I won't stand here and let you treat me like shit just because I walked away from you."

"It has nothing to do with me." I throw my hands up

in the air. "But it has *everything* to do with that little girl standing across the room, and that's why I'm speaking to you like this, Addison. Nothing has ever been about Sailor. She was a *baby*. You don't know what we went through after you left! You didn't deal with the long days and nights I spent consoling a screaming infant because she wanted her mother. *You* abandoned her, and for that I will *never* forgive you." I start pacing in front of the kid-sized table, infuriated beyond belief but doing my best to keep as much of a level-head as possible because Sailor's in the room. "So yeah, forgive me for having a fucking attitude toward you. You want to stay? Then stay. You want to rebuild what you tore down with Sailor? Be my fucking guest, but you'll do so under my supervision and rules. Keep my personal life out of it, though, because as far as I'm concerned, the Addison I knew became a ghost the second you walked out the door and left your ring on the table."

She stands in front of me with her mouth agape, staring at me like I slapped her. Verbally, maybe I did, but it feels great to finally get that off my chest. For a brief moment, I feel guilty, though.

Maybe I was too harsh.

But then I remember watching the heart of a barely one-year-old shattered into pieces because of *her*, and I feel like my wrath isn't even close to the intensity it should be.

Done with this conversation, I shake my head and

leave the room, wanting to put as much distance between me and Addison as I possibly can. I can't promise I won't say something that I will come to regret one day, or that Sailor will overhear more of this conversation that she already has.

Wandering back toward the kitchen, I set off in search of Hailey, wondering where she is. The couple of rooms I check are empty, but when I go into the kitchen, I catch a flutter, her red hair as it dances in the wind outside.

I find her out on the back porch, sitting on the top stair with her head in her hands. A lump forms in my throat. I can't even imagine the thoughts going through her mind, or her reaction when Addison showed up.

I hate that I wasn't here to intervene.

"Hey," I say gently, sitting next to her.

She turns her head, her red rimmed eyes glistening. "Hey."

Seeing her so upset feels like a knife being twisted in my gut. I have no clue what Addison said, or did to make her so upset, but the fury ignites within me and I want answers.

"Sweetheart, I'm so sorry." I wrap my arm around her, pulling her into me. She lays her head on my shoulder.

"Did you know she was coming?"

"Of course not." I kiss the side of her head. It's a relief to have her in my arms, but fuck, I need to make this right. "She's been calling, but by the time I finally decided to call her back, she didn't answer. I thought she was just being persistent—figured she saw one of those videos online, and decided to stick her nose where it didn't belong. Which is what she did, but I didn't think she would just show up."

"She was in your house, Declan. When I came back from dropping Hartley off at the airport, Addison was already inside and sitting at the kitchen table."

My shoulders slump. "I didn't even realize she still had an extra key."

"Look, Declan, I know—"

My heart plummets. "Whatever you're about to say right now, just stop. Don't let her get into your head."

I look down at her, to see her lashes filled with tears. "Easier said than done."

Gently grasping her chin, I tilt her face up to look at me. "Sweetheart. Tell me what she said to you."

"Nothing really. Of course the things she said were snarky, but she's Sailor's mother, Declan. Can I really blame her for being a bitch to the woman in her house, helping to care for her daughter?" Her voice breaks. "She doesn't know me."

"And Sailor doesn't know *her*. Addison lost her right to call herself a mother the second she walked out the door and never came back. She has no right to speak down to you, and I have absolutely no problem telling her that. This also isn't her house, sweetheart. Never has been."

"I don't wanna make things more strained with your

family. Sailor deserves to have both her mother and her father and I can't get in the way—"

"What family, Hailey? My family is Sailor, and now, *you*. Addison sure as shit isn't a part of that. You and Sailor are the only people who matter. I don't give a shit if Addison thinks I'm being a dick. She doesn't have the right to show up on a whim, let herself into *my* home, and be rude to my girlfriend."

A small smile appears on her face. "Your girlfriend? Is that what I am?"

"No, sweetheart, you're so much more than that, but for fear of scaring you off, we'll leave it at the girlfriend title for a while." Bringing my lips to hers, I kiss her. It's soft and brief, but now doesn't feel appropriate to kiss her as passionately as I'd like to, even if I do feel the need to remind her how much she means to me.

"You can't possibly mean that," she whispers, looking at me wide-eyed. "We've only been dating for a week."

"What can I say? I'm a man who knows what he wants, sweetheart. And trust me when I say my ex isn't going to get in the way of what's developing between us. I'd never allow her to."

Hailey snuggles deeper into my side and sighs deeply. The whirlwind of the last hour or so replays in my mind as I start to process everything. Nothing about Addison showing up makes any sense—the only logical explanation is that she saw one of the videos of me and Hailey and is using it as her attempt to have success at fame.

Wrapping my arms around Hailey, I rest my head against hers and we listen to the sound of the birds chirping. My backyard offers a moment of peace before the storm returns the moment we walk back into the house. I stand firm on what I said—I'll never let Addison get between us. We have something incredible, and I'll protect it with everything I have.

But while I sit here and hold her, a jarring realization hits me like a Mac truck. How far is Addison willing to go to get what she wants? I might not let anything get between us, but what if Hailey does?

CHAPTER TWENTY-TWO

Hailey

It feels like forever since I've been at my own house, surrounded by things that are solely mine. But the silence is deafening, and even though I've only been here a few hours, I'm not enjoying the alone time. Sailor's laughter isn't coming from the next room. There's nothing on the TV to keep me company. I tried to play music on my phone, but even that didn't breathe life into me like it normally does.

Staring at my reflection in the mirror, I put my diamond stud earrings on. I'm all dolled up and ready to go on a date with my *boyfriend*. I should be more excited, but I just feel so unsure.

It's been a week since Addison showed up, and even though Declan put her up in a hotel so she wouldn't be tempted to be at his house all the time, I haven't stayed over either. Her coming back has put distance in my heart.

Logic tells me he doesn't want her. His words and his actions say the same, but just knowing Sailor's mother is back in the picture so soon after we've started our new relationship together has me retreating.

I'm not intentionally withdrawing, but I also don't want to be the woman standing in the way of them reuniting their family.

With that being said, I can see right through Addison, even though she puts on a sickeningly sweet persona in front of Declan. Acting like a perfect woman, a perfect mom, and even pretending like she's a perfect "friend" to me while he's around. She smiles at all the right times, laughs in all the right places, but when he's not present, her glares are menacing, her words are cutting, and the seeds of doubt she's planting in my mind are growing faster than ivy.

I hate it. I hate it so much because I know in my heart Declan cares about me, and that my bond with Sailor is *strong*.

But I still can't help feeling like the other woman—a mistress in *their* relationship. The engagement ring may be gone, but the ghosts of their past float around haunting Declan's home, whether he wants them there or not.

Tonight, though, Declan says is all about *us*.

He's taking me out again, this time to a ritzy seafood restaurant, then a walk through downtown Bridge Point.

It's a far more public setting than we've gone out in

before, and for some reason that feels monumental. Like he *wants* to be seen with me.

Like I said, his actions are reflecting his words, and while that should be reassuring, there's still a pit in my stomach.

I want to be with him, and I want things to work out between us so badly, but there's two people in a relationship, and it's not just about what I want. And my lack of self-confidence loves to tell me he'll eventually leave me for her.

Choosing a deep crimson lipstick, I paint it on my lips, pursing them after it's applied. Pushing open my closet doors, I grab a flowy black dress and pair it with my favorite strappy sandals to make it feel slightly more casual.

The clock on my phone reminds me Declan should be here any minute, so I toss my makeup back in the bag and go wait in my small living room. The tick of the clock echoes through my home, and I lean against my couch.

Scrolling on socials, I input *baseball kiss* into the search bar, pulling up countless videos of me and Declan. Watching them makes me feel better—it's easy to see the chemistry between us—it serves as a good reminder to ground myself and stop letting *her* win.

I'm giving Addison exactly what she wants. She's inflicted doubt. Uncertainty. She wants to weasel her way back into Declan's good graces, and presumably into his bed.

Am I really going to let her?

Declan is a man worth fighting for, and she didn't. She did the opposite and left without a word.

She doesn't deserve him.

A knock on my door has me jumping, straightening upright. A rush of excitement floods me, and I swipe my clutch purse off the side table, tossing open the door.

Declan stands there, leaning against my doorframe, looking amazing in a light blue button-down shirt that's rolled to his elbows, and a pair of dark wash denim jeans. His unruly hair is slicked back, and his beard has been trimmed.

"Hey, sweetheart," he greets, handing me a bouquet of pink peonies and baby's breath.

"These are beautiful. Thank you." I lean my face down into them and smell their soft fragrance.

"Of course. How are you?"

Moving into my condo, Declan follows me into the kitchen so I can put the flowers in water before we leave. "I'm okay," I tell him honestly. "Excited to go out tonight."

"Me too," he agrees with a grin. "It's high time I wine and dine you."

"You spoil me enough as is, but I am pretty excited to check out this restaurant."

A few minutes later, we're in his car, driving through

the neighborhood. With his hand on my thigh, Declan grips the inside of it as he drives with one hand.

"Are you ready for this weekend?" The Bears have a game tomorrow night against the Rocky Mountain Raptors—finally, their first home game.

"Yeah. I think the guys have it in the bag. The Raptors are good, but we're better." He gives me a wicked grin, and I see the playfulness in his eyes.

"I can't wait to watch," I tell him earnestly.

Sailor and I will be there tomorrow and to my dismay Addison brought it upon herself to accompany us, squealing when she realized friends and family get to sit in the VIP boxes by the dugouts. Declan isn't pleased she's coming, but she flies out the next morning so he's humoring her.

The rest of the car ride is short and silent. When we pull up in front of the restaurant it's packed with people dressed to the nines, flooding out onto the street. I feel underdressed, but everything I read online said this wasn't that fancy of a restaurant, so maybe there's some sort of special event happening.

Finding a place to park is a challenge, but we're able to find a space a couple blocks over. Declan parallel parks perfectly, and comes around to open my car door, extending his hand so I can take it.

Playfully, he holds our hands in the air and encourages me to do a twirl. It's lighthearted, and we both laugh.

When we start walking down the street, he immediately switches sides with me, making sure I'm on the inside, and he's on the outside. It's a small gesture, but one that means a lot—I know that's not something a lot of men do anymore.

By the time we're seated at our table, both our stomachs are rumbling, and everything on the menu looks delicious.

"I'm not gonna lie," he says, still looking down at his menu. "I was hoping for an empty restaurant and a corner booth so I could push you past your comfort zone a little."

My eyes snap to him. "And what exactly do you mean by that?"

He flashes a toothy smile, and shrugs, pretending like his words mean nothing, but the underlying meaning of them makes my thighs clench beneath the table, heat rushing both between my legs and up to settle on my cheeks.

When the waiter arrives, I order the lobster mac and cheese, and Declan gets the surf and turf platter. We talk about everything under the sun, making small conversation and having fun. It renews a sense of comfort in me, and I needed that so badly.

My cheeks hurt from laughing, and dinner is delicious, but while we're waiting for the check to arrive, I notice a group of people a few tables down from us staring and making gestures in our direction.

I feel my face fall.

Declan turns, following my line of sight. "What's wrong?"

"They're talking about us." I'm openly staring at them, letting them know I see them.

From my peripheral, Declan shrugs. "Let them."

Once the bill is paid and we're back in the evening air, he takes my hand in his. Bridge Point has a beautiful downtown, with old-fashioned gas lamps that line the street, and benches everywhere. String lights twinkle as we stroll down the sidewalk.

"Do you want to get dessert?" he asks as we pass an old-fashioned looking ice cream shop.

I shake my head. "Maybe on the way back. I'm so full right now."

"Alright, sweetheart." He pulls me closer and presses a kiss against my hair before dropping his arm over my shoulder.

Finally, we make it to a small park and he leads us to an empty set of swings. We both take one, and I let my feet drag in the sawdust while the creak of the chains floats through the air.

"I haven't been on a swing since I was a kid," Declan muses. "I used to swing as high as I could, and then jump from the top. I'm surprised I never busted my ankles, because that shit was rough landing." He laughs at the memory, and I just know a wave of nostalgia has hit him.

Nostalgia.

Does he feel nostalgic having Addison around this week, too?

I can't imagine he hasn't thought about when they were together, and a happier time for their family, when Sailor was a baby.

As my mind wanders back to the thoughts I've tried so hard to push away, I find myself retreating again.

This time Declan notices, too. "Where'd that pretty mind of yours just take you, sweetheart?"

Giving him a small smile, I shrug. "My intrusive thoughts are working against me."

"What are they saying?" he asks gently.

"That you and Addison deserve a chance to make things right again, for Sailor's sake. She's the mother of your daughter, and I can never compete with that. Maybe she really does still love you."

"The *only* thing you just said that's true is that she's the mother of my child," he stresses. Hopping off his swing, he comes to stand in front of me, pulling my hands from the chains, holding them in his. "She's trying to become an actress, and that's exactly what she's doing. Acting. She's trying to manipulate us. I promise you she doesn't care about me, she just cares about furthering her own career, we both know she saw that video of us and thought to herself 'hmm, maybe I can spin the narrative'. There's not a genuine bone in that woman's body, I can promise you that, sweetheart." Bringing my hand to his lips, he kisses the back of it. "I don't want you getting cold feet about us, because I can't express enough how much you mean to me."

"I just feel like maybe you need to give it a chance, Declan. Maybe this time she's being honest." I hate every word as it leaves my lips but what else am I supposed to say? I'm torn between desperately wanting him, and wanting to also believe the best in people.

"I won't." His voice is firm, unwavering, and his gaze heated. "Even if you and I weren't together, I would never give that woman a second chance."

"I just want you to make sure you're making the best choice for you, and for Sailor." My heart splits in two, and I know this is from my own doing. "Your family deserves that."

"I know I am, and I'm going to prove it to you, sweetheart."

"Declan—"

"Consider this the first night of me showing you how badly I want this until there's not a single doubt or hesitancy in your mind."

He pulls me off the swing and I stumble into his body. Holding me tightly, he tips my head back and kisses me.

We kiss like teenagers under the moonlight until we're both breathless.

Sliding his hand down to mine, he nods to the street. "Now c'mon. I want to buy my girl some ice cream."

CHAPTER TWENTY-THREE

Declan

"Alright, Coach, I'm all for polyamory, but it doesn't seem you're like you're the type of guy who'd be down. Care to share why there's two women in the VIP box making eyes at you across the field?"

"That's Sailor's mother," I grit, answering Austin.

Looking over my shoulder, my jaw clenches as my gaze connects with Hailey's, and I immediately lose some of the tension I'm carrying. Leaning against the railing, she looks out at me. She's stunning, wearing one of my extra Bears hats and a red T-shirt.

Behind her, Addison sits with Sailor, also looking at me. My jaw clenches again.

Whipping my head back toward Austin, I huff.

"You good, Coach?" Gareth asks, jogging up to us. His brows furrow with concern.

"Yeah, I'm fucking good. This has just been a hellish week."

"Why'd Sailor's mom show up all of a sudden? I thought she was out of the picture?" Gareth asks, but then adds, "Sorry if that's overstepping. You don't have to talk about it."

"All good," I tell him, and glance back over at Hailey. "She showed up out of nowhere. She won't admit it, but I suspect it's because of those videos. She thought if she tried to win me back, it would be *her* getting the attention."

Both Gareth and Austin look at me with a *what the fuck* look.

"She left us to go pursue a career in Hollywood," I explain further.

"Ah." Austin nods his head. "That makes so much sense. She's chasing clout."

"She sure is," I agree in a growl of annoyance.

"How's Hailey handling it?" Gareth asks, glancing around the field.

The stadium is starting to fill up—the game starts within the hour.

"I'm not even sure I can give a confident answer. It feels like she's been withdrawing, and rightfully fucking so. But at the same time she's still present and gritting her teeth through it."

"She's a fucking champ." Austin laughs.

"You can say that again."

"You think she'll get fed up with the baby mama drama?" Austin asks curiously, stretching out his arm.

"God, I fucking hope not. If she walks out of my life, I swear." I shake my head. "I don't know how the hell it happened so quickly, but I've definitely fallen for her. And since everything else has been such a public spectacle, I figured the best way to prove myself to her is in another public way. To make sure she knows I'm serious."

"Oh yeah?" Gareth says, surprised. At the same time, Austin asks, "What's the plan?"

Looking back over at Hailey again, I smile when our eyes connect like magnets. Like they always do, because we're meant for each other. "You'll see in about fifteen minutes."

CHAPTER TWENTY-FOUR

Hailey

With a small, final wave in Declan's direction, I turn and go back to my seat, lowering my baseball cap further while I avoid Addison's watchful eye.

The heat is blistering, making me grouchy, or maybe that's a certain ex-fiancée that keeps lodging her way beneath my skin. Her snide comment from earlier echoes through my mind as I attempt to smooth my hair, the humidity making it more unmanageable than it already is.

I know I should play nice with Sailor's mother, but I have no interest in speaking with her. It's hard to be around a bully, especially one who's an adult. But in less than twenty-four hours she'll be gone, and I'll be able to process everything that's transpired this week.

Things have been moving so quickly with Declan, and being forced to work through the situation with Addison while still trying to figure out what we mean to each other, has been a challenge, to say the least.

This morning she cornered me in the kitchen while Declan was packing things into his truck, and suggested that I stay behind.

"There's no need for a nanny today, Hailey," she sneers, waving her hand dismissively in front of me. "You can take the day off. Perhaps some time for yourself wouldn't be a bad option—you could stand to get your hair done."

For a second I'm too stunned to speak, then my brain catches up. She's such a vile woman. "Oh, Declan already told me I wasn't on Sailor duty today! I'm going to the game because he wants me there, not because I'm required to be there."

Then, he walks back into the house and straight to me, kissing me on the side of the head. "Alright, I'm headed out. See you there, sweetheart."

Declan glares in Addison's direction, before walking out.

I resist the urge to laugh.

"I wonder what people must be thinking," Addison snarks the moment my butt hits my chair. Having Sailor between us isn't nearly as big of a buffer as I need for this woman.

Just a few more hours and she's gone.

I know better to engage, but at this point, I relent. "About what?"

I wonder if she can hear the exasperation in my voice.

More of the team's family and friends start filling the seats in our box, saying hi to me as they pass by. It's satisfying that no one is saying a word to Addison, though.

Yes, I can be petty sometimes.

"Well, it's obvious Sailor is my daughter. She looks just like me. It doesn't take much for people to put two-and-two together. And since you're here, I can't imagine the things that must be going through their head about *you*."

This. Horrible. Woman.

"I'm sure they're not thinking anything, Addison. I've met these people several times. They know I'm Sailor's nanny." *And something to Declan*, but I don't add that in.

She cackles like the witch that she is, rolling her eyes. "Yes, the *nanny*. So funny how you were hired to care for our daughter, and now you're sleeping with *him*."

Her insinuation flares something ugly inside me, and I'm about to fire back, when Sailor's sweet voice says, "Mama, I have cotton candy, please?"

Both mine and Addison's attention pulls to Sailor, and it's only then that I realize she's looking up at me, tugging on the hem of my T-shirt.

She called me mama again.

She called me mama in front of her mom.

With wide eyes I look up at Addison, who's seething. Her cheeks have turned red, whether from anger or embarrassment I'm not sure, and she looks like she's ready to reach right over Sailor's head and throttle me.

Ripping Sailor's hand from the bottom of my shirt, Addison completely pretends like the question wasn't directed at me and says, "Of course you can, sweetie." Then, over Sailor's head, she shakes her own, lowering her voice as she looks me dead in the eyes and spits, "You're a fucking whore. First you steal my fiancé, now my kid?"

Guilt slams into me, knowing that's exactly what she thinks. In her mind, I'm the villain, and in mine, she is.

It's a sad, disappointing way for two women to view each other—we should be coming together over our mutual love of Sailor if nothing else, but I know from many years of studying people, children, and families, that we have a long road ahead of us before we ever get to that point.

A response is on the tip of my tongue when suddenly Declan's laughter radiates through the stadium. My head whips up to the Jumbotron, and I find his handsome face broadcasted across several screens.

Excitement clashes with the sadness and soon my stomach explodes with butterflies. I'm in love with this man, and I love his daughter like she's my own.

The realization hits me hard.

Grinning like an idiot, I watch as *Coach Declan Lane* flashes across the screen, accompanied by music and several shots and videos of him coaching the Bears, before it changes back to the interview of him.

"Coach Lane," a female voice booms across the

stadium. "You've had quite a big season already and it's just beginning!"

"You can say that again," Declan agrees, nodding along with a smile on his face.

"What would you say the highlight of it has been thus far?"

"Watching the Bears take home that opening weekend victory is up in the top three, for sure." The pride radiates off of him through the screen, making it palpable throughout the stadium. Everyone seems to be focused on the coach's words.

"Top three?" the interviewer asks with curiosity. "You're talking about that viral video, aren't you? What's it sitting at now? Twenty-two, twenty-three million views?" she teases. "Is that your number one highlight of the season so far, Coach Lane?"

Declan shakes his head. "Nah, Ma'am, you've got it all wrong. It wasn't the videos, although, I guess that's not entirely true." Declan grins—no, beams at the camera. "My top highlight of the season so far was what you can call a curveball in my personal life. I never saw it coming."

My heart begins to thunder, mouth slightly agape as I watch the screen intently.

"And that was?" she eggs him on.

At this point I'm at the edge of my seat, wondering where he's going with this. It has something to do with me, and part of me is nervous as hell.

Okay, all of me is nervous as hell. My palms sweat, my foot bounces against the concrete in anticipation.

Staring directly into the camera, he tells the world, "I hit a home run in love and fell for my dream woman, Hailey Shea."

My jaw hits the floor.

Cheers erupt through the stadium along with a collective round of *aww's*, but the rumble of excitement in our VIP box screams the loudest. At the same time, I hear Addison curse with a whole slew of profanity, and not subtly, either.

Red and pink hearts pour onto the screen as the music from earlier starts to play again, quickly fading into a different song as a new Bears player is featured.

I stare at it for several seconds, completely speechless and in a trance, until my focus shifts, and I scan the field for Declan.

He loves me, too?

Declan loves me.

And he just broadcasted it in front of thirty-thousand people and God knows how many viewers across the country.

"*I'm going to prove it to you, sweetheart.*" His words from earlier play back in my mind.

My eyes keep scanning the field and the dugout. Standing, I look everywhere I can think of, but come up empty. *Where is he?*

More cheers erupt around us, coming from the stands closest to the VIP box, and instinctively I follow the energy. Turning, and tuning Addison out as she whines, "You've got to be kidding me."

Taking the stairs two at a time, Declan gallops down them, his eyes never wavering from me. I blow out a shaky breath, completely frozen in the middle of the landing.

"Daddy!" Sailor squeals, but for once, her mother does something right and holds her back.

Declan doesn't stop until we're chest to chest and he's crowding my space. My back bumps into the railing at the same time his hand tangles in my hair. With his other hand, he uses his finger to push my hat up, so he can see my eyes.

Searching them, we stand there staring at each other, neither of us saying a word, just lost in the moment.

I can't believe he just did that.

I can't believe he's not on the field right now—the game is literally starting without him.

Finally, as the unmistakable sound of a ball connecting with a bat ricochets through the stadium, he rumbles, "Hi."

His thumb brushes back and forth against my cheek, as I burst into laughter. "Hi."

"I'm not usually one for big, publicized gestures, but seeing as we've gone viral twice, I thought we could do it one more time, for old time's sake."

"Well I certainly think you've succeeded. That was....I'm not even sure I have words for what that was right now. I'm still trying to process. You love me, Declan?" I still can't believe it.

Me.

This phenomenal man loves *me*?

"More than I ever imagined loving anyone in my life," he tells me earnestly. "I know it's been alarmingly fast, Hailey, and this might scare you off, but—"

"No," I cut him off. "It's been fast, but at the same time, it's been tortuously slow."

"Understatement on the torture part, sweetheart. I've wanted you for a long time, I just needed to step out of my own way and allow myself to love you. And I really hope you start to believe how much you mean to me, since I just confessed my feelings in front of thousands of people."

"I love you," I proclaim, wanting him to know without a doubt that his feelings are reciprocated.

"God, I've been wanting to hear that for too long." Taking my mouth with his, he kisses me eagerly, and once again the crowd around us goes crazy, no longer focusing on the game, but on the coach.

The cheers continue and his tongue swipes into my mouth as he deepens the kiss, claiming me for all to see. Pulling apart, we both smile into it, and Declan lifts his fist into the air in a victorious motion.

"I love you too, sweetheart. Unfortunately, though,

now I have to go coach these goofballs. But mark my words, when we get home—"

Pushing up on my tiptoes, I kiss him again, then lower my voice to make sure he's the only one who will hear me. "When we get home you're going to coach me through a home run. How's that sound, Coach Lane?"

"It sounds like the beginning of a beautiful season, sweetheart."

CHAPTER TWENTY-FIVE

Declan

Four Weeks Later

A sharp *boom* slams behind me, pulling my attention away from the barbecue and over to where Hailey sits at the patio table. Her phone's face down, her hand still resting on it, and it looks like she's trying her damndest not to cry.

Closing the lid on the grill, I go to her. "What's wrong, sweetheart?"

She looks up at me, her eyes sparkling with unshed tears. I hate being right sometimes. Placing my hand on her back, I begin to rub it gently.

"Hartley's flight was canceled. She can't get another until tomorrow morning."

Hailey's been dying for her sister to come up again, and she's been so excited to have her here for our first hosted event as a couple. Although it's just a small barbecue with Gareth, Jensen, and Austin, she was looking forward to Hartley being here, too.

"That's okay. We'll get her in the morning." I try to console her, but the glare she sends in my direction tells me I'm not helping much. Leaning toward her, I kiss her on the tip of the nose. "First I'll take you to that coffee shop in Ridgewood you love."

"I just miss her." Hailey sighs.

"I know you do." Through the open windows of the house, we hear the doorbell ring. "Keep an eye on the grill?" I ask, passing her the tongs.

With a quick glance at Sailor, I confirm she's still playing happily in her sandbox, then I go inside.

"Damn, Declan, I knew you were loaded but this house is something else." Austin pats my shoulder as he walks into my home. Gareth and Jensen file in behind him, both of them stopping to shake my hand.

"Do you want us to kick off our shoes?" Jensen asks, lingering in the doorway.

"Nah, it's fine. We're headed outside, anyway." Locking up behind them, I gesture to the kitchen where the French patio doors are open. Through them, there's a clear view of both the barbecue and Hailey, who's now walking in our direction with a smile on her face.

"There's the woman of the hour," Gareth greets, pulling her in for a hug.

Austin hugs her next, but not before extending his hand to spin her around. "Lookin' good, Hailey. Don't you have a sister? You should set me up."

"I have a twin," she emphasizes. "But sadly, she's taken."

Austin beams. "Sadly? Sadly sounds like it could work in my favor."

"I think her boyfriend would have something to say about that," she says with a hint of sass in her tone.

"Oh yeah," Austin taunts, "and who's her boyfriend?" He smirks like he actually has a chance with Hartley, whom he's never seen a picture of, let alone met.

That should raise my hackles since he assumes they're identical, which means he could potentially be attracted to my girl, but it doesn't. Austin wouldn't stand a chance with a woman like Hailey—he's far too goofy.

"Owen Marsh." Hailey shrugs. "I actually really don't like the guy, but she doesn't listen to me."

"Your sister is dating Owen Marsh?" Jensen speaks up from where he's lingering in the doorway. His eyes narrow in a lethal gaze.

"Yeah, why," she asks, not having a clue about their background. I never told her about their history simply because it's never become the topic of conversation at any point.

Walking closer to the rest of us, Jensen focuses his gaze on Hailey, although it's slightly softer than before. "Owen

Marsh is possibly the biggest piece of shit I've ever met in my life. I sure as hell wouldn't want him dating my sister."

"Trust me, I don't, but it's not my decision. Hartley is a grown woman, she can do what she wants."

Jensen just shakes his head in response, and I see my opportunity to guide the conversation in a different direction.

"Well, on that note." I pull open the lid to the grill, the smell of barbecue immediately wafting out. "Who's hungry?"

"Starving." Gareth pats his stomach appreciatively, reminding me of a childlike move Sailor would do. "What can I do to help?"

"Everything's pretty much done," Hailey interjects. "But I'll run inside and grab the cold stuff."

"I'll give you a hand," Austin offers. "We can talk more about your sister."

Laughing, Hailey shakes her head and leads the way back inside.

Jensen passes me a platter from the table, and I load chicken and bratwurst onto it. "Thanks."

"No problem."

When we're all settled in the warm evening air, our plates are full, and we fall into a comfortable small talk.

"So when's the next viral video?" Austin asks playfully.

"I think our days of viral videos are behind us."

Hailey's gaze meets mine. "I'm not interested in any more than five minutes of fame."

We've had several long conversations about Addison and her role in Sailor's life moving forward. She opened up about her insecurities and everything that Addison did and said to her while I wasn't around. I confessed my fear of her leaving me and Sailor, and how I knew it would destroy us both.

In the last four weeks we've been raw, open, and vulnerable with each other, laying a solid foundation that I hope—I know—will last a lifetime.

And now that the buzz has worn off about my over-the-top grand gesture, Hailey and I are falling into a comfortable normal day-to-day routine.

She hasn't moved in yet, but I'm hoping that's going to happen very soon. I might even ask her tonight, if the timing is right. She's been spending more and more nights over here, and it just doesn't make sense for her to keep paying for her place.

The conversation shifts over to the Bears season and the guys get heated in a good way, talking about who they want to take down, where they think each other can improve, and what players from other MLB teams they'd trade for if given the opportunity.

Hailey puts a plate of freshly baked chocolate chip cookies down on the table, winking in my direction, and

I'm instantly transported to one of the first nights I realized how utterly captivated I am by her.

"Pretty sure you two shouldn't be allowed to bake again. If this is what happens when there are cookies, I can't imagine what the kitchen would look like if you girls baked a cake," I tease.

She shrugs. "You won't be saying that after you taste my cookie."

The shade of crimson that painted her cheeks after that is something I'll never forget.

"Damn, these might be the best cookies I've ever tasted," Jensen compliments, completely unknowing the inside joke between me and Hailey, and I practically choke on mine.

Across from me, Gareth leans back in his chair, pulling his cell out of his pocket. "I'm sorry, I have to take this. Hello?"

Standing, he moves a few steps away on the porch. "What? Indy, slow down. What's wrong? What? I'm on my way. No, just stay where you are. I'll be there soon."

Frantically, he hangs up and shoves his phone back into his pocket. "I've got to go, I'm sorry."

"Is everything good?" Austin asks, concern swimming across his features. "What's wrong with Indy?"

Who's Indy? I think to myself, the name sounds strangely familiar.

"I don't think so. Thank you guys for dinner."

Quickly, he leans down and presses a friendly kiss to Hailey's cheek, then touches my shoulder in passing before he runs out of the gate in my backyard.

"Fuck," Jensen mutters, looking over at Austin.

Feeling like I've missed a conversation somewhere along the line, I raise my eyebrows. "Who's Indy?"

"You remember meeting Dylan at the pre-season team barbecue? Gareth's best friend?"

"Oh, I do!" Hailey perks up, and my memory's jogged, too.

"Yes." I nod, encouraging him to continue.

"Indy is his sister. Gareth's been in love with her for forever, but Dylan is absolutely oblivious."

"Oh, damn." I rub my beard, letting my thoughts take me back to conversing with Dylan. He did seem a little lacking in the common sense department, still though, he was a nice guy.

"Yeah. Oh, damn," Jensen repeats.

"Hope she's okay," Austin adds, then for a second the table goes quiet.

"Can I have another cookie?" Sailor asks, breaking the silence, but not waiting for me or Hailey to say yes before she stands in her chair and grabs one off the plate in the center.

Her innocence makes us all laugh, and like Sailor, we all end up reaching for another cookie, too.

"Well, that went off with only a minor hitch." I wrap my arms around Hailey as she works on the dishes at the sink. I got Sailor bathed and tucked in for the night, and now all that's left to do is finish cleaning up the kitchen before I can have Hailey all to myself.

I can't wait to have my second dessert.

"For the most part," she agrees. "I hope Gareth and his friend are okay though."

"I'm sure they are. I'll message the group later," I reassure her, kissing her neck.

She hums a moan as my hands begin to wander along the front of her body.

"You spending the night again tonight, sweetheart?"

"If that's okay with you." She turns the water off when my fingers play with the button of her jeans. Drying her hands, she tosses the towel on the counter then leans her head against my shoulder.

"It's always okay with me. In fact, I'd prefer if you never left. Move in with me."

Turning within my hold, she faces me, looping her arms around my neck. "You want to live with me?"

"Is that such a surprise? You're here all the time, but there could be more of you. Touches of Hailey all over the house. Your feminine touch around the place. My space becoming our space. You already have a key, sweetheart, let's just get your belongings over here too and make it official."

"This isn't too fast for you?" If I had a nickel for every time she voiced concern about things moving too fast for *me*, I'd probably be a billionaire by now.

"Nothing with you is too fast, Hailey," I assure her, like I do every time. "I'd toss you over my shoulder, throw you in the car, and drive your ass to the courthouse now if you'd let me."

"You don't mean that." She laughs, pushing onto her tiptoes and planting a chaste kiss on my mouth. It immediately prods the fire inside me, making it roar to life.

Using my hips, I pin her body to the counter, grinding my erection against her so she can feel exactly how much I do. "I mean it with every bone in my body, sweetheart, but if you need me to keep reminding you, I will every day for the rest of my life."

Her hands sink into my hair, and I groan at the feeling of her touch. "Do you promise?"

Nuzzling my nose against hers, I close my eyes, letting every memory we've shared in the last four months flood my thoughts—every lingering stare, every subtle touch. The late night talks, the embarrassing moments. The way my heart beats out of control when she's around, and the way my life became exponentially brighter when she entered it. Even if Hailey and I had never become romantically involved, I can say without a shred of doubt I would have wanted her in mine and Sailor's lives forever.

So now, when she asks me if I promise to remind her how much I love her every day for the rest of our lives, my answer is simple. Concise. And it comes without hesitation. "Yes, sweetheart, I promise."

EPILOGUE

One Year Later

The early spring sun beats down on the VIP box at Coit Stadium, an unseasonably warm day even hotter with the heat reflecting off the metal seats.

It's opening day and the Bears are playing against the Rebels for the second year in a row. The confidence of the guys has been sky high after winning the World Series last year, despite the few small hurdles along the way.

This year, they're hoping to take home that title again, convinced that if history repeats itself and they beat the Rebels in their first game, they'll have it in the bag.

Either way, I'm so proud of them—especially Declan. He worked so hard last season while still being the most attentive partner, and an amazing dad to Sailor.

Things with Addison are still pretty heated, but we're

working on it for Sailor's sake. Somewhere between Sailor's birthday and Christmas, Addison realized I wasn't going anywhere, and finally decided to play *somewhat* nice when she showed up for another visit.

Scanning the field for Declan, I'm surprised to not see him, but wave to Gareth instead.

Turning my focus to Sailor, I hand her a package of opened fruit snacks, then get comfortable in my chair, taking a swig from my water bottle. As I'm crossing my legs, the Jumbotron starts playing a montage of Declan.

A smile upturns my lips as I watch the amazing collage of photos and videos they've collected, and I'm transported back to last year when he told me he loved me on this very screen.

"Coach Lane!" a woman's voice projects through the screen. I think it's the same interviewer from last year, but I'm not positive. "How are you? Ready for opening day?"

"I'm doing well, thanks for asking. And yes I am. Excited to kick off another great season coaching this amazing team."

"A great season seems to be an understatement coming off of last year. It was quite a triumph! You got the team, the trophy, and the girl, if memory serves."

I gasp, my mouth immediately popping open in surprise. *Did she really just say that?*

Declan laughs. "Yeah, you're right about that. I'm a lucky man."

"I guess you can say you got everything you hoped for last season, isn't that right?"

Scooting to the edge of my seat, I cling to their every word, completely surprised that this interview has taken such a personal turn.

Declan scratches his five o'clock shadow—his beard growing back slowly after he spontaneously shaved then Sailor and I begged him to grow it back. "Well, not everything."

The screen glitches, black and white scratches flickering through it.

"Oh?" The interviewer laughs, her vocals the only thing projected through the stadium.

The screen flickers back to life only to show Declan standing, before it cuts out again.

Looking around, I see the other friends and family members just as confused as I am.

Declan's voice booms through the stadium. "Yeah, I've actually been meaning to do something, but haven't found the right way to yet."

"What's going on?" someone from behind me asks.

"I guess the Jumbotron's malfunctioning?" a man answers.

The screen then roars back to life, but this time the interview with Declan is gone, and the cameraman pans throughout the stadium, zooming in on fans who are cheering and excited to be shown on the screen.

"Well, there's no time like the present," the woman's voice echoes again, despite not being on the screen.

"Yeah, you're right," Declan agrees.

I suck in a sharp breath when my face fills the screen, the camera landing on me, but it's what's behind me that catches me completely off guard and takes my breath away.

How had I not known what was happening? How were people not screaming and tipping me off?

My hand flies to my mouth as I turn around in my seat to find Declan down on one knee on the stair behind me, holding a sparkling princess cut diamond ring.

I sink to my knees in front of him, and he reaches out to cup my face with his free hand. His finger brushes away the tear that rolls down my cheek.

"Hailey Nicolette Shea, every monumental moment we've had so far together has been in a stadium, so I figured this next one should be no different. Baseball has had my heart for as long as I could remember, until you walked into my life and flipped everything upside down. Now *you* have my heart, and I never want you to give it back. Would you do the honor of making me the happiest man alive and marry me?"

"YES!" I cry, then don't waste another second before pressing my lips to his. "Yes," I repeat over and over, peppering kisses to his mouth until finally he wraps his palm around the back of my neck and keeps me there, kissing me deeply. "I love you, Declan."

"And I'll continue to spend every day proving to you how much I love you, sweetheart. I hope I'm succeeding so far."

"There shouldn't be a doubt in your mind that you are." We both look down at the shimmering ring as he slides it on my finger, rubbing his thumb over it.

"It's beautiful," I whisper, completely enamored by this entire proposal.

"So are you." It's only then, when he kisses the side of my head, that I register the roar of the crowd, and that we're still projected on the screen.

Following my line of sight, Declan laughs at what I know is a horrified look on my face. "Trying to have us go viral again?" I shake my head, bringing my fiancé back in for another kiss.

He laughs, and against my lips he murmurs, "Seems like a trend with us, sweetheart. Might as well keep it going."

And just like I suspected it would, our proposal goes viral.

Forty-six million views and counting.

Thank you for reading Stealing Forever! Your reviews are important, please considering leaving your review of Stealing Forever on Amazon.

Can't Get Enough of the Bridge Point Bears?

Gareth's book, Stealing Kisses is up next!
Preorder your copy!

Curious about what Hailey was reading to Declan?

Live out your fantasies in Only One Night, where you can become the main character in this unique Halloween novella.

Still craving more A.R. Rose books?

Dive into Marked By Cain to meet Indy: Ex-Boyfriends brother, second chance, motorcycle club.

Or grab Wreck Me, where you'll catch a glimpse of the Bears team owner, Blake Bradley: New adult, rich girl/poor boy, insta-love, light suspense.

ACKNOWLEDGMENTS

Every year during baseball season I think to myself, man, I should really write a baseball book. This year, that thought snowballed and as I sat at a game on opening weekend, an entire series was dreamt up.

Thank you to all of my amazing readers who have stuck with me through the beginning and continue to read my books even though each book is vastly different than the rest.

To the new readers just discovering me, buckle up buttercups! Thank you for being here!

To my wonderful team who helped push me along, cheered me on, and helped shape this story to what it is today. My alpha readers, my amazing editor, and my wonderful proofreaders. I appreciate you all more than you know.

Thank you to my family and friends for always being the biggest supporters in my life. Love you guys.

And finally, an extra special thank you to all ARC readers and influencers on my team who always show their love and support.

A.R. Rose's greatest job in life is being a mom to her two boys. She is a born and raised California native who loves to hang out at home with her kids and her dog.

A.R. realized her passion for writing in the third grade, although it wasn't until early 2022 when she began to pursue it. Now, if she skips a day of writing, she feels as though her day is incomplete.

On any given day, you will find A.R. toting around her laptop and her Kindle, with a coffee in hand, daydreaming about the characters and worlds she's building. She is grateful to have the opportunity to bring her stories to life and is excited about her journey as a romance writer.

CONNECT

Join A.R. Rose's newsletter for info & updates

https://www.authorarrose.com/email-subscribe

Website

www.authorarrose.com

Reading Group

https://www.facebook.com/groups/authorarrose

Facebook

https://www.facebook.com/authorarrose

TikTok

https://www.tiktok.com/@authorarrose

Instagram

https://www.instagram.com/authorarrose

Continue reading for a peek of an ex-boyfriend's brother, Motorcycle club romance, that'll keep you on the edge of your seat!

Marked by CAIN

A.R. ROSE

🏍 Ex-boyfriend's brother
🏍 Small Town
🏍 Motorcycle Club
🏍 Redemption
🏍 Second Chance
🏍 He Falls First

CHAPTER ONE

Rosie

SIX YEARS AGO

"I'm not sure what you're not comprehending, Rosie. You either get a fucking job and throw down on a portion of the rent, or you find somewhere else to stay. It's not like you're doing anything else to help us with this fucking house." Brent slammed the dresser drawer shut, smashing the arm of a t-shirt as he did. My boyfriend was such an asshole—so hot and cold about literally everything.

"You can stay here as long as you need, babe."

"Don't worry about rent, babe. Focus on finding a job."

My plan was never to stay here permanently, but I needed more time to get on my feet. I just moved here because of him. We weren't serious enough to move in together, but a fresh start sounded like exactly what I needed, so I figured, why not? I'd get a studio, find a job, screw my boyfriend.

Life would be easy.

Except it wasn't. Finding a job was proving to be a little more difficult than I had initially thought, but it was fine. I just needed to lower my standards of where I was applying.

Once I did, I had three interviews lined up. One of them was bound to hire me. *Hopefully*.

The grocery store would, no doubt. Who got turned away by a grocery store?

It'd been two months, and I didn't want to be in Brent's bed every night any more than he wanted me in it. We had a very... relaxed relationship. And by relaxed I mean, we played the part of boyfriend/girlfriend when we felt like it but weren't so serious that we were discussing solid plans about our future.

And before you go chastising me and thinking, *'but Rosie, you moved for him'*, just remember, I moved for *me*. He just happened to present me with a place to stay and a crutch to lean against as I got settled.

Brent and I were not headed toward Mr. and Mrs., that was for damn sure.

Sounds awful, right? I did love Brent. I just didn't see us growing old together. He was my right now, not my forever. There was a difference.

"Why would I help with the house when I'm not the

one who makes the mess? I keep my shit clean. It's really not that hard, Brent. You and your brother should figure out how to do the same."

"You're such a fucking bitch sometimes, you know that, right? I think I've been more than fair to you, Rosie, and I'm done with you and your games."

I rolled my eyes and glanced down at my black-painted nails in boredom. "Yeah, yeah, Brent. Done with me until tonight, when you beg me to spread my legs."

"I don't beg for shit."

"Keep telling yourself that. I'll keep them closed for a while and we'll see how long you can hold out for."

"You think I won't go elsewhere?"

"Don't care."

"We'll see how much you don't care later when I make your ass sleep on the couch and you have to listen to me pound into someone else through these paper-thin walls."

"Go for it. I'll just crawl into your brother's bed," I spat, my heart skipping a beat at the very thought of it.

See, while I may have met Brent first, it was hard to deny the attraction I had for his brother.

Brent was your classic all-star, preppy, clean-cut, boy-next-door. The type who was the perfect person to bring home to your parents and start making lifelong plans with.

On the outside.

On the *inside*, he could be a real-fucking jerk. Like,

want to scratch his eyes out and punch him in the nuts, kind of jerk.

It was baffling how he'd somehow wormed his way inside of my heart.

We'd been together for over a year now, if you don't count the month we were broken up. I *did* care about him. Honestly, what we had worked for us. And when he wasn't being a raging dickwad, Brent was actually very sweet and attentive. We had fun together. High highs. Low lows.

Toxic, I know. What I just described was practically the definition of a walking red flag.

But again, it worked for us. It worked for *now*.

Brent was a few years older than me, and the type of relationship he wanted was one of convenience and fun. It was a relationship I knew I could easily give him, because in return he could give me the sense of stability I craved. I was a little wild, I knew it and owned it, and I needed a person in my life to ground me—balance me out. Most of the time, he gave me that.

It also didn't help that Brent was pretty damn hot. But while he had the boy-next-door vibe, his brother was his polar opposite...the bad boy. Two years younger, rough around the edges, and devastatingly, ruggedly, gorgeous. Even his name was as sinful as he was—*Cain*.

He was covered in tattoos—which really matched my

energy—and he didn't give a fuck about anything or anyone.

Actually, the only thing he did give a fuck about was Brent.

And *me*.

Which was a real bitch since I was technically with his brother.

Cain and I just connected better than Brent and I did, though we never crossed *that* line. But man, if you could actually fuck someone with your eyes, there wouldn't be a time or a place he hadn't taken me. Many late nights were spent in each other's company, talking about anything you could imagine. Our guards had come fully down, and I honestly wasn't sure anyone knew me better than he did. So many times I'd thought about telling Brent we were finished. I was hopeful I could leave him and one day move forward and be with Cain.

But Cain was never willing to let it happen.

Because I was his brother's girlfriend, I was off-limits completely. He'd never disrespect his older brother like that—which was wildly disappointing for me. I wasn't a cheater, and I never would be, but if Cain asked me to leave Brent for him, I wouldn't think twice.

Hell, if Cain asked me to leave Brent in general, I probably would.

I cared about Brent, I truly did. I loved him. I just

wasn't sure if I was *in love* with him. How could I be when my heart beats for another man? His *brother.*

"You think crawling into my brother's bed is a threat? Cain is loyal to me, Rosie. He'd kick you out on your ass faster than you could blink," Brent spat, dropping onto his bed and crossing his legs at his ankles. He locked his hands beneath his head, his elbows sprawled, looking as relaxed as could be.

"I'm not sure why I bother with you, Brent. But I'm over this bullshit. You asked me to move to this freaking city with you, knowing I wouldn't have a job or a place to live. I'm done. Find yourself some other girl to fuck with." Lucky for me, my suitcase had never been unpacked because the jackass didn't have extra space for my shit in his dresser. All I had to grab was my phone charger and bathroom stuff.

Walking across the hall, I grabbed my makeup and hair care products, cradling them in my arms as I made sure I didn't leave anything behind.

I wasn't positive where I'd go tonight, but I'd figure it out. I always did.

Tossing everything into my suitcase, I zipped it up and expanded the handle to roll it out. "Last chance to be a gentleman, Brent."

"Nah," he said without looking at me, pulling out his phone.

My eyes narrowed into slits and my head bobbed as I

watched him scroll mindlessly as though I wasn't even in the room anymore. Tilting the suitcase, I rolled it behind me as I walked out of his bedroom.

The hallway was dark, the house quiet, as I moved through the small space toward the front door. When I reached for the knob, a deep voice sounded from the shadowed living room beside me.

"Rosie," Cain called. He sat on the couch in the dark, his face illuminated by the soft moonlight flowing in through the window.

"What, Cain?" What was there to even say? His brother was in the next room, probably listening for the sound of the door closing. This wasn't the first time we'd broken up, or the first time Cain had wanted to say something as I walked out the door after a fight with his brother. But like every other time, Cain said nothing and stared at me from his spot on the couch, his eyes blazing with unspoken words. The rigidness of his features told me he had heard mine and Brent's exchange and he hadn't liked what he heard.

Turning my head back to the door, I twisted the knob and walked out.

When it closed behind me, I didn't bother looking back. Instead, I held my head high and walked down the path, using my key fob to pop open the trunk of my car. The sound of small rocks crunching beneath the wheels of my suitcase battled against my heartbeat that echoed in my ears.

I was so frustrated with Brent and how I let him toss me to the side *again*, and how Cain let his brother treat me like shit and didn't speak up, *again*. I guess it wasn't fair of me to act like Cain really had any authority to say anything, but what woman didn't want a knight in shining armor on occasion? I guess I wouldn't be getting that from either of the Michaels brothers.

"Rosie!"

Maybe I spoke too soon.

Cain's voice cut through my inner battle with myself as I tossed my suitcase into the trunk of my blacked-out Honda Accord.

"What do you want, Cain?"

"Come back inside. Please."

"For what? So Brent can give me more details about how he's going to screw someone else and have me listen? Or so you can sit silently while he talks shit? As much as I love being the source of your entertainment, I think I'll pass." I slammed the trunk harder than necessary and rounded the car, pulling open the driver's side door—but I didn't get in. Like a true glutton for punishment, I watched him from over the roof of the car, waiting for him to say something.

Cain rubbed his tattooed hand across the back of his neck, looking down at the ground. After several tense seconds, he brought his attention back to me. "Where are you going?" he asked, taking a few more steps toward my car.

"I don't know," I admitted, my eyes narrowing as I tried thinking about where my first stop would be. Probably the motel on the outskirts of Ridgewood. It'd be the most inexpensive. My heart hammered in my chest as I made a snap decision to pull down one more layer of vulnerability I couldn't really afford to gamble with. "Come with me."

Cain's eyes darkened with my request, and instantly I could see the turmoil behind his light brown eyes. "It's not that easy. Brent's my brother..."

"He'll get over it," I argued, doing my best to keep the desperation out of my voice. I knew I was walking a fine line between being vulnerable and being desperate. I *wasn't* desperate, but Cain held a piece of my heart in his hand and I'd be lying if I denied that I wanted him to run away with me.

"We both know he wouldn't, he'd—"

"Cain? The fuck are you doing?" The screen flew open and hit against the side of the house as Brent's voice boomed from across the front yard. Cain's spine went ramrod straight.

Brent's eyes bounced between me and his brother, narrowing as he assessed us, drawing his own conclusions. Being unapologetically myself, I tossed him a snarky smile, knowing he was about to either explode on both of us, or turn around and slam the door in our faces.

Cain turned to face his brother, shrugging nonchalantly. "She ran from the house like a bat outta hell. I came to find out why."

"Not so sure it looks that way from where I'm standing, *brother*."

Resting my hands on my hips, I watched the two men face off, one looking skeptical while the other looked like he was trying to come up with an iron-clad excuse to save his own ass.

"Not sure what you think it looks like, but I was just making sure your bitch knew to respect our property next time she walked out of the house. She slammed the door so hard it rattled the front windows," Cain spouted, the lies tumbling from his mouth effortlessly as he turned back to me and his features hardened.

"She isn't my bitch anymore," Brent scoffed, stomping down the two steps of the weathered front porch. "Kind of seems like you want her to be your bitch, though."

A satisfied smile curled at my lips—my earlier suggestion of crawling into Cain's bed had clearly resonated with Brent. It got him thinking. Doubting himself and his brother's loyalty.

My intention was never to cause a rift between them, but rather remind Brent that being in his presence was *my* choice. Despite my current lack of income, I knew my damn worth, and with the snap of my fingers, I could have another man lined up if I wanted.

My smile was short-lived though, because nothing could have prepared me for Cain's response, and the wound it would ultimately leave on my heart.

Cain tossed his head back and laughed. What was normally a rare, yet beautiful sound with the power to inflate my heart, came out villainous and cruel. "Why the fuck would I want your sloppy seconds, Brent?" His eyes connected with mine as he delivered the final blow that would ricochet through my darkest moments for years to come. "She's nothing but damaged goods. Trailer trash. You couldn't pay me to give her my cock."

I knew words could hurt, but I hadn't realized just how badly until then.

Without hesitating, I flung myself into the driver's seat and cranked the ignition, not bothering to let it warm up before I tossed the car into drive and sped away, my tires squealing against the asphalt. I blew through the stop sign at the corner of their street, needing to get as far away from the Michaels brothers as quickly as I could. It took everything I had not to glance in the rearview mirror as I hightailed it out of their neighborhood and in the direction of the most expensive hotel in Ridgewood.

Forget staying at a cheap motel. I had some money tucked away, stashed because my subconscious *knew* something like this could happen, and I couldn't think of a more perfect reason to pull a little cash out.

A high thread count and some room service would be exactly what I needed while I licked my wounds for the night.

Why would I sit around in a crappy room and dwell on the words of two certified jerks? Tomorrow was a new day with back-to-back job interviews and a whole lot of promise for my future.

Glass half full, right?

Fuck Brent, and fuck his brother even more.

I was Rosie Adler, and if there was one thing I'd learned over the years, it was that the only person on this planet I needed was myself.

Certainly not a six foot four, tattooed, sexy as sin man who looked like he could murder your enemies with his bare hands, but around you was a complete marshmallow.

Definitely *not* Cain Michaels.

CHAPTER TWO

Rosie

PRESENT DAY

"*Fuck*, mia preferita, you feel amazing," Sly grunted as he slammed into me, his beautiful Italian accent even thicker during sex. He reached his large hand up and kneaded my boob. "God, I'm so close. I don't think I can hold it much longer. You...feel like paradiso."

My legs wrapped tighter around his body and joined at the ankles as I attempted to shift the pressure to stimulate my clit. Not that I hadn't already orgasmed. But twice never hurt.

Sly's grunts and groans filled the air as he drilled into me, a thin layer of sweat coating his back like he'd been running a marathon. We'd only been at it for less than five minutes, but his chest heaved with exertion.

I did my part in letting out small moans at the right

times, digging my nails into his back. I was good at pretending to be super into it—I'd had enough practice at faking it over the years. Thankfully, Sly couldn't see me rolling my eyes and glancing at the diamond Rolex I hadn't bothered taking off when we got naked.

It wasn't his fault I was bored. My head wasn't in it—I was tired and stressed, more in the mood to be alone than to be naked and sweaty, but I'd hoped a good romp in the sheets would take my mind off the world around me.

Two more grunts and a slam later, Sly's rutting was over. His body fell to a heap on top of mine and I allowed him around sixty seconds of caressing before I gave him the boot. "Alright, Sly, off."

His gaze slid to mine as I stared up at him. He smirked, dipping down to kiss the side of my mouth, his dick twitching inside of me before he slid out. He rolled off my body and dropped onto the bed.

"Sorprendente," he muttered, his voice soft. Bastard had already tossed an arm over his eyes as if he was going to fall asleep immediately.

I reached over to pull a cigarette off the nightstand and lit it up. The cherry glowed red as it caught, and I tossed the lighter aside. Filling my lungs, I let my eyes close as I willed myself to relax.

Anxiety crept into my chest, sitting heavily. No sooner had I inhaled a second puff, Sly pulled it from between my lips and stuck it between his.

This was our ritual. We fucked, played pass the cig, and we passed out.

Well, correction, he passed out. Some nights I laid there for hours until I fell asleep. Other nights, I left and went home.

It wasn't that I didn't enjoy being with Sly, because I truly did. He was great. There was nothing I could pinpoint that made me dislike him, which was why I couldn't figure out why my feelings for him weren't stronger.

Being with him was easy and secure. At all times, I knew where I stood with him and after so many failed relationships, a man like Sly was exactly what I needed. A great lover with a wicked tongue, easy on the eyes, and extremely compliant. Whatever I wanted, I got—the man had never so much as thought the word no when it came to me.

It didn't hurt that he also looked hot as hell in his black jeans and leather vest. Just seeing him on his motorcycle, his bronzed skin covered in tattoos, his dark hair always combed to perfection, and the way he could wear a pair of dark aviators, was enough to get me wet.

I never would have guessed I'd be into the whole motorcycle club thing, but here we were. The best part— Sly never tried to lock me down. He took me at face value and never forced me to commit to a label I wasn't interested in. I wasn't his girlfriend; he wasn't my boyfriend.

The simplicity of our arrangement was what kept me from going stir-crazy.

Finishing the cigarette, I watched Sly peel the condom from his limp dick, knot it, and toss it onto the nightstand next to its wrapper. My face contorted as I outwardly cringed, grossed out that he just tossed it haphazardly onto the same surface he puts things like his phone on.

And *he* made fun of *me* for taking a disinfectant wipe to everything the second I stepped foot into his room. I wasn't a germaphobe, but bikers—*men*—could be absolutely fucking disgusting.

I kept my mouth shut and made a mental note to wipe it down at some point while settling into the softness of the cotton sheets. As my eyes shut, I felt his hand circle my middle, and he pulled me closer. There would be no falling asleep for me. His body heat was stifling.

His arm draped across my naked tits, while he gripped my waist and tucked me into his body. *Little spoon.* All I could think about was rolling out from under his grasp.

I *hated* cuddling.

After what felt like hours, the steady rhythm of his breathing told me he was finally asleep. Peeling his fingers from my areola, I scooted my body away and silently placed my feet on the cool hardwood below. I sat for a minute, listening to the low snores as they fell from his lips.

I really did like the man, but there was just something

lacking that I couldn't put my finger on. Sly was all golden retriever vibes. And there was nothing wrong with that. Wasn't that what most women wanted? A loyal, loving man who spoiled them? I should want that too.

Maybe the problem was me.

Retrieving my thong, bra, and the men's button down I had worn as a dress today, I quickly got dressed, leaving the shirt unbuttoned. Grabbing another cigarette and my purse, I headed for the door. As I slipped through the crack just wide enough for my body, I lit up another smoke. The cherry was the only illumination in the dark hallway, and as the door clicked closed behind me, I leaned against it with my eyes shut, enjoying a drag.

"That shit will kill you, Rose."

His voice made me jump, not realizing someone else was in the hallway with me. I turned my head to the right where his voice had come from, and watched him push off the wall and stalk toward my direction.

Stopping in front of me, he plucked the cigarette from between my fingers and carelessly tossed it to the floor, snuffing it out with the sole of his boot. "You need to fuckin' quit."

"And you need to quit stalking me, Cain," I retorted, crossing my arms in front of my chest. His eyes trailed down my body, appreciating the swell of my tits, the curves of my wide hips, and the lack of thigh gap. All so different from the body of the girl he once knew.

The Rosie I had been...the Rosie I was...she wasn't me. She was the shiny exterior I showed the world, but I was tired of being her.

While some old habits die hard (and are super challenging to let go of), I was able to control my body.

Life had been crazy over the last two years and I'd decided I needed a change.

Oh, who was I kidding? My life has always been crazy, and I was constantly making changes to myself. But it was within the last couple of years, while watching two of my best friends find their happiness, I realized *I* wasn't happy.

Growing up, my biggest hardship was low self-esteem and an unhealthy relationship with binge eating. Eventually, I fell into the other extreme and became good friends with a little plague called the starvation diet. I trained my body to survive on water-based foods and extremely lean proteins (every once in a while) while I also obsessively killed myself in the gym.

For years I was a slender little minx, but it cost me my happiness.

I conformed to what I thought I needed to look like for society—what I needed to look like to fit into my "bad girl reputation" I had so eloquently placed upon myself. Slender. Dark hair. Big tits. Tattoos.

For what?

That was the million dollar question, and let me just tell you, it wasn't worth a goddamn penny.

Once I had my come to Jesus moment and realized I didn't need to be anyone other than myself, I said goodbye to the salads I forced down my throat and reacquainted myself with carbs. And if people didn't like it, they could promptly fuck off.

Then, I spent a small fortune at the salon to turn my jet-black hair back to my natural—*or as close as I could get to it*—brunette. I even treated myself to a few extra tattoos, because why the hell not?

Instead of a size four, I was now more of a comfortable eight/ten, and I loved myself more than ever.

So when Cain's gaze finally reconnected with mine, I jutted my chin out with confidence and gave him my award-winning attitude. "Why the hell are you out here? Enjoying the audio-version of the porn you'll never get to watch?"

His smirk made my stomach turn. The jury was still out on whether it was a good "butterflies" type or bad "want to upchuck all over him" type of turn.

Probably a little of both.

Cain, unfortunately, caused the butterflies in my stomach to flutter whenever I caught sight of him, which seemed to be more frequent lately. He'd aged like a fine wine. Thirty-five years old and a fine specimen of a man. He was covered head to toe in black and gray tattoos—at least I was sure he was. I hadn't ever seen him completely naked, but had seen him without his shirt many, many times. He had that rugged appearance that made my toes curl. His coffee brown hair was always messily pulled back into a bun at the crown of his head, and his facial hair was always scruffy, but in a way that worked for him. He had the zero effort thing down and in his favor. Add that to his blue jeans, t-shirt, and leather vest decked out with club insignia—*damn*, he was fine.

An ass, but pretty to look at.

"Hearing you *fake it* was the highlight of my night, Rose," he told me, his voice thick with sarcasm.

I flipped him the bird before pushing off the door I still leaned against. Giving him my back, I walked down the pitch-black hallway. Not many people were up in the bedrooms yet, it was hardly midnight, but Sly and I had snuck off earlier in the night. The vibration from the bass of the speakers rattled the walls from the music playing in the bar on the floor below us. "Stop calling me Rose," I called over my shoulder.

Cain's footsteps were heavy behind me as he followed. "Where are you hurrying off to?"

I took the opportunity of being cloaked in darkness to button my shirt. My feet were bare and I moved quietly, but he was hardly three steps behind me. When I made it to the back staircase, I stopped and turned to him, turning on the fake charm. "What do you want, Cainy-boo?"

I ran my finger down the soft leather of his vest and along the waistband of his jeans. My sarcasm didn't go unnoticed, and he boxed me in, caging me as my back pressed against the cool wooden banister.

"You know, *Rose*, your attitude isn't as off-putting as you think." He traced his nose against my cheek, tipping his lips toward my ear. "I *see* you," he whispered softly.

My body betrayed me, and a shiver ran over my skin. The cocky bastard knew it too, because he added, "I know this isn't one-sided. You're just fucking around with Sly and buying time until I finally claim you."

"You can't claim a woman who wants nothing to do with you, Cain."

"Your body seems to disagree with that statement."

"It's cold in here, asshole. My goosebumps are for lack of warmth, not lack of dick. We both know I'm not lacking in the latter, so just go ahead and fuck off back to where you came from."

He tipped his head back and released a husky laugh. "Hell hath no fury like a woman scorned, right, Rose?"

"To have fury toward you, Cain, would imply I care. Which I don't. Truly."

"Your words pain me, baby."

"Actions speak louder than words, Cain. Although you seem to have a knack for making your words pretty damn loud."

His features turned dark and his mood sobered. No longer smirking and laughing, I could see the fire behind Cain's eyes as he searched my face, looking for a glimmer of sarcasm or playfulness to indicate I wasn't being serious. But I was.

I forced myself to hold my own, to mask the feeling of inadequacy threatening to show on my face. As memories pushed their way to the forefront of my mind, I could feel the hurt surfacing.

No.

I looked away, but something must have trickled across my face, causing Cain to take a step back. "Rose, you know I didn't mean what I fucking said. I had to say it to save face in front of Brent."

Whipping my head back toward him, I snarled, "You knew how I felt about you, Cain. And you knew how he treated me. Yet you still sat there and called me—*to my face*—what was it again? Damaged goods, trailer trash? Wait... No... That wasn't all you said."

"You know I had to. If he knew I was after his girl, he would have murdered me. He would have murdered *us*."

"Bullshit, Cain. Brent and I were so on-again off-again, he wouldn't have cared either way. When I walked away from him for good last year, he didn't come running. Plus, *we* never did anything. You and I were nothing but unexplored feelings and lustful looks across the room. It's never been about your actions. In this case, Cain, it was about *your* words. How *you* treated me. I expected better from you. You were always the nice one."

"He's my fucking brother, Rose. What was I supposed to do?"

"It doesn't matter what you should have done, because you did nothing. And now, I want *nothing* to do with you. I've let it go, Cain. Moved on. You should too."

Without waiting for his reply, I ducked beneath the arm keeping me caged against the banister, and took the stairs down two at a time, not sparing him a backward glance as I pushed open the door to the main floor of *my* bar, Andromeda.

www.ingramcontent.com/pod-product-compliance
Lightning Source LLC
Chambersburg PA
CBHW021022310726
48969CB00006B/1500